ABOUT THE AUTHOR

David Whately-Smith was born in 1949 in Lymington, where he has spent most of his life. He was educated at Lancing College and Exeter University where he studied German and French. His father was headmaster of Hordle House School, a co-ed prep school in Milford-on-Sea.

After working for Courage Brewery for fourteen years, he joined the family business in 1986. He spent thirty years at Hordle House, which merged with Walhampton in 1997, becoming Hordle Walhampton, and, eventually Walhampton.

During his career, he taught mostly French and History. He retired in 2016.

He married Penny in 1982 and they have two children and, at the time of writing, three grandchildren.

Silent Heroes is his first novel.

Silent
Heroes

David Whately-Smith

Printed and bound by CPI Group (UK) Ltd, Croydon, CR0 4YY

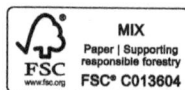

MIX
Paper | Supporting
responsible forestry
FSC® C013604
FSC
www.fsc.org

This book is dedicated to the memory and courage of
Freddie and Myrhiam le Rolland and the townsfolk of
Moussey.

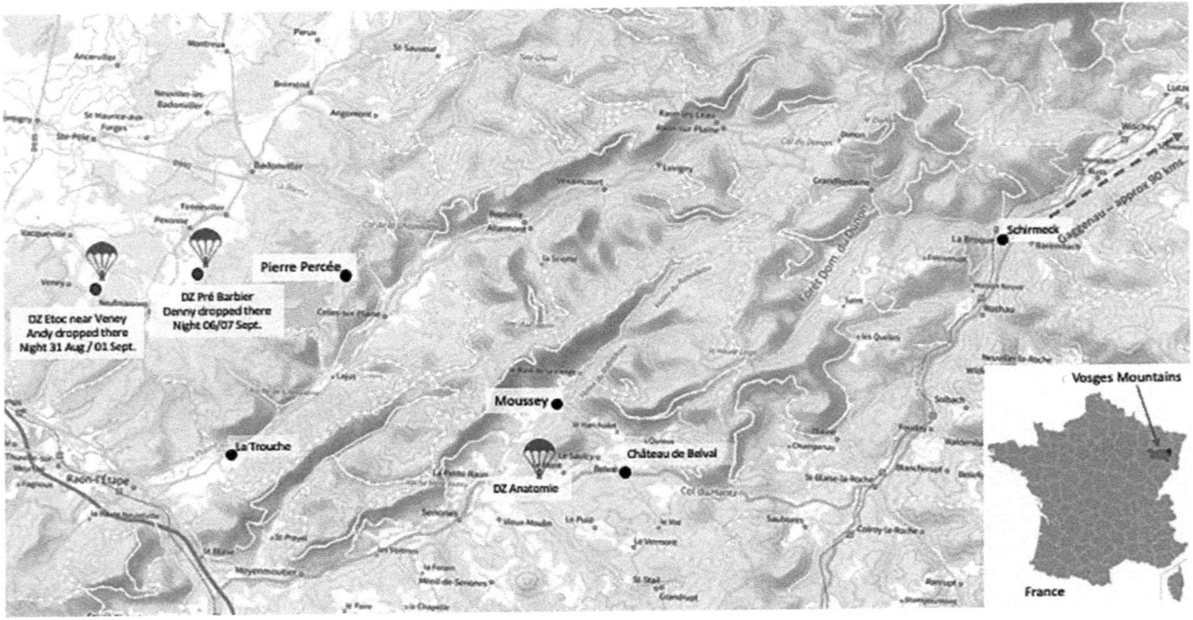

DZ Etoc near Veney
Andy dropped there
Night 31 Aug / 01 Sept.
DZ Pré Barbier
Denny dropped there
Night 06/07 Sept.
Pierre Percée
La Trouche
Moussey
DZ Anatomie
Château de Belval
Schirmeck
Gaggenau – approx 90 kms
Vosges Mountains
France

Operation Loyton area (August–October 1944)

Chapter One

The room in which I sit and write these words overlooks the yard at the back of our farmhouse, where the chickens scratch around in the dirt. Over the past few weeks, I have watched the old rooster as he becomes slower and scrawnier, shedding more and more feathers, and the irony is not lost on me that he is the one my wife named 'Xavi'.

The fact is, that in these last strange months, my life feels more in its evening than it ever has. I'm more conscious of the ache in my bones when it's wet (which, unfortunately, here it often is), of the tremor in my fingers, of the long shadow that time leaves behind itself. Yet in some ways, it's the most alive I've felt in years. Perhaps that's normal when a creaking old Frenchman is confronted with his ten-year-old self.

Since the Englishman knocked at our door, the words of my father's favourite writer, Monsieur de Maupassant, have been in my mind: that the memory is a more perfect place than the universe; it gives life back to those who no longer exist. And in casting my mind back to the events of that summer nearly eighty years ago I am reminded of just how imperfect this universe can be and what – and who – it can take away from you.

Yet writing these pages has brought life back to certain people – people who deserved to have much more of it. More than I have had, maybe. Had I been more than a boy, I would have had the same terrible questions asked of me, but how would I have answered them? I cannot say.

That morning a few months ago, my eighty-first birthday as it happened, dawned like any other in our little village in the Vosges Mountains in Eastern France. My wife, Mathilde, was busy after breakfast trying to unravel the mysteries of the bewildering new radio my son had sent me for my birthday. I had just been outside to check on the weather, given the dog a run and taken my daily medicine: a deep breath of fresh mountain air. I whistled an old tune as I hobbled up the hill to feed the hens. That afternoon my friend from the next village would be taking me fly fishing (the one true love of my life, my lady wife excluded) on the lake across the valley.

I was just taking my box of flies out of the shed when there was a knock on the door. The dog immediately started going at it. 'Quiet! Sorbet,' I shouted. Sorbet gave me a lugubrious look and slunk back to her basket.

'Chérie, if that's that fool Noirtier again, please tell him we don't have his damn hose.' Mathilde's sigh spoke volumes as she went to open the door.

A moment later, she called out that it was someone for me. 'A strange looking man. I'd say English or American, judging by his fashion sense. Maybe he's here to sing you happy birthday', she murmured as I passed her on the way to the front door.

She was right. Definitely not a Frenchman. The stranger was balder than me, a little stooped, wore jeans and trainers and carried a leather satchel. He stepped forward and gave an eager Sorbet a pat.

'Monsieur, I am very sorry to impose on you, but you are Xavier Le Rolland?', he asked in decent French.

'Yes, I am. I don't know what you want but we are very busy,' I replied, shunning his proffered hand.

'Can I come back when it is convenient?'

'What's it about?' The man's persistence was becoming a nuisance and I was already thinking about whether to take my dry flies or streamers for the trout.

'It's a bit of a long story.' he said.

'Come on, you want to sell me a vacuum cleaner? You want me to find Jesus? Spit it out, man.'

'Well, I've come from England.' he went on. 'Specifically, to visit this house, Monsieur.'

I looked at him as though he was completely mad.

He cleared his throat. 'I'm trying to trace what happened to my uncle, and I know he was here in this village in September of 1944. What I am hoping to find out is if you have records of who was living here at that time.'

It took me a moment to register what he said. Then it hit me like a freight train. My heart started thudding in my chest so hard I wondered if he could hear it. 'Go on.' I urged.

'He and his wounded companion took refuge in this village, and, we believe, were helped by the couple living in this house.'

'Your uncle's name?' I asked, betraying nothing of what I felt.

'His name was…'

Suddenly I could see a ghost of his impish expression in the man's face.

'Andy' I whispered, to his astonishment.

***

I should go right back. It was in the middle of August 1944, some two months after D-Day, that things around here began to change. Up until now we and our fellow residents of the villages in this part of the Vosges had been largely cut off in our mountain retreats from the effects of the war. I was ten, and the only visible inkling I had that France was involved in any sort of conflict came on still and clear days when the echoes of trains carrying military vehicles and other tools of war reverberated from the valleys below. Up above too, streams of aircraft flew day and night towards Germany to bomb hell out of the German factories and cities, as my father put it gleefully. Otherwise, life had seemingly continued much as normal. At the beginning of it all, some of my friends' fathers had gone to join up. Not all had returned. Those that did were badly affected by their experiences and seriously chastened by the ease with which the Wehrmacht had swept the French Army aside in 1940.

However, as the history books will tell you, by August 1944, the Wehrmacht was no longer the force it once was. Hitler had invaded Russia in June 1941. His blitzkrieg tactics had resulted in huge swathes of Russia being captured very quickly. Joseph Stalin, their leader, galvanised the Russian people into a desperate and ultimately successful defence of their homeland. The Germans lost huge amounts of men and weapons during the campaign.

Stalin had been begging his American and British allies to ease the pressure on his armies by opening up a second front and invading France. So, on D-Day, 6th June 1944, the invasion of France commenced. By nightfall, more than 150,000 Allied troops had landed on the beaches of Normandy.

Hitler and the German High Command realised that once the Allies got ashore and consolidated their positions, the war would be lost. In order to defeat the Americans and British on the beaches, Hitler transferred many divisions from Russia to France. He now had his hands full with fighting on two fronts.

While the Allies did reach land, the battle for Normandy was fiercely fought for some twelve weeks with huge numbers of casualties on both sides but ultimately the sheer fire power of the Allies told, and the Germans were forced to retreat. The British headed north to liberate Belgium and Holland, while the Americans under General Patton headed east. With the Germans in headlong retreat, his armoured columns covered huge distances each day until he paused close to the German border towards the end of August 1944. His supply chain was by then some five hundred kilometres long.

So it was that our little rural backwater was soon to be flooded with troops as the region was prepared for defence against the Allied advance. The inconceivable was about to happen. Situated as we were so close to the German border, the Reich that Hitler had bragged was going to last for a thousand years was about to be breached. It was going to be the mother of all battles. News had reached us that British paratroopers had landed in advance of the American attack. Their mission was to report on the enemy's dispositions, attack targets of opportunity (railway lines in particular) and generally create mayhem.

As a result, the Germans were not just preparing for the American onslaught but also hunting down the paratroopers who were making a real nuisance of themselves by launching attacks and detonating explosives before disappearing into the vast pine forests that covered the mountains. Little did we know it at the time, but we were about to have first-hand experience of both and rather sooner than expected.

They arrived the next day in our little village and set up their headquarters in the ruined castle, which occupied the heights with a commanding view of the surrounding area. Their arrival did have one advantage as far as I was concerned. Generally, the local schools had been taken over by the German military for barracks, storage areas or headquarters leaving no premises in which to conduct lessons and so school was suspended. Quel dommage!

A typical ten-year old, I woke early with excitement. The unexpected holidays could go on for a while. I lay in bed thinking about the possibilities of the next few weeks. As soon as I went downstairs, however, I could tell that something in the house had changed. My mother was not humming as she went about her daily chores. Her face looked a little strained as she peeled the potatoes. From his downstairs bedroom, I could hear Papa groaning and muttering to himself. I knew they were as pleased as I was about the unexpected bonus of extra holidays and the prospect of having me around more than normal – or at least Mama was – so what was the matter?

'What is it?' I asked.

My mother frowned and let out a long sigh. 'My darling boy, we've been lucky that the war has passed us by so far. But I'm afraid it's all going to feel rather close for a while. We've just been told that from tomorrow we must have two German officers to stay in our house.' With that the tears started, and she reached for her handkerchief.

Life would never be the same for me, my mother, my father. And our dog.

***

The Vosges were near the border with Germany, more hilly than truly mountainous, and dotted with villages like ours, some quite remote. The hillsides were densely forested, riddled with crags and rocky outcrops and man-made paths on which it was easy to become disorientated.

These tracks were primarily used by the foresters to harvest the trees, which were then transported to the many sawmills down in the valleys. Forestry was the main employer. My father, Freddy, and my uncle, Gérard, had their own sawmill in which Papa was the principal investor. The business provided a steady income, until Papa's horrendous accident changed everything.

He had been covering for one of his men who was off sick when a badly stacked pile of logs collapsed on him, crushing his leg, and giving him a nasty blow to the head. As a result, he was not able to work and could only walk with the greatest difficulty. Worse still, the mild brain injury had left him moody and unpredictable. Whenever he looked at himself in the mirror, he would always be met by a reminder of the day that ruined the rest of his life. The log had made a terrible mess of his mouth and his teeth. The dentist, a friend of his with a strange sense of humour, gave him a legacy and his trademark, a shiny gold filling in one of his front teeth.

This happened when I was six years old, so I can remember some of what Papa was like before his accident. The burden that my Mama had to carry while bringing up a young son and at the same time looking after a bad tempered, invalid husband would for most mortals have been intolerable, but Mama saw her role as full -time carer for Papa as a role given to her by God.

Both my parents were Parisians. Mama trained as a nurse in one of the well-known hospitals, while Papa grafted his way to success as a businessman. They decided to move to the Vosges, having made visits to Gérard,

Mama's brother, and Aunt Camille, who lived in the pretty village of Moussey. Mama moved to a hospital in Raon l'Étape to become head nurse. I appeared somewhat unexpectedly and rather late in their lives.

Mama's nursing expertise proved invaluable when Papa had his accident, but it meant she had to give up her job too. Papa sold his business stake to his brother-in-law, allowing them to afford a comfortable home. However, the unexpected expenses of making it accessible for Papa's mobility challenges disrupted their financial plans. As a result, Mama had to adopt a frugal approach to spending.

Little wonder, therefore, that my mother should be reduced to tears by the prospect of two more mouths to feed – and German ones at that. She had been told that German officers billeted in local houses handed over credit notes to cover the cost of board and lodging, but these were not worth the paper they were printed on. Stories abounded of ladies of the house presenting such notes at headquarters being sent packing.

Papa, who had not been old enough to fight in the Great War, had lost two uncles in the slaughter. The area in which we lived had historically been part of Germany and so you couldn't always be totally sure where people's loyalties lay. However, no such doubt persisted with Papa. He already hated the Germans before the fall of France in 1940. That hate had now turned to vitriol. The constant mutterings and colourful language would make for some interesting evenings at the dinner table with our house guests, I thought to myself.

Despite the unreliable mountain signal, Papa found

solace in the radio, one of his few sources of enjoyment. Just as profound gloom settled over him after France's fall, his spirits had lifted in recent months. News of German retreats and defeats brought renewed hope. Regular visits from Monsieur Mercier, an old friend from their sawmill days, provided updates through his limited English and BBC broadcasts. Papa learned of the successful invasions by the Americans and British, leading to the liberation of an unexpectedly intact Paris. Later, they would discover that Hitler's general had defied orders to destroy the city during the German withdrawal, adding to the resilience and triumph amid the chaos of war.

For the first time in a long time, Papa had a smile on his face. However, he did say that things would change round here soon, even in our isolated valley, as the war crept closer towards us and the German border. And the Germans were a cruel and ruthless occupying power. As a ten-year-old boy, I didn't know whether to be excited by the thought of soldiers and guns in our village or terrified by what it might all mean.

The first day of the holidays was the biggest anti-climax I had ever experienced. I wasn't allowed to go fishing, but instead had to help Mama get the rooms ready for the German officers. Mama and Papa both slept on the ground floor because Papa could not manage the stairs. On the first floor there were three bedrooms and a bathroom. I was moved to a smaller bedroom at the end of the corridor, so I would be well out of the way of our so-called house guests.

I could tell that Mama was anxious about how Papa

would react in the presence of the 'grey lice' or 'les sales Boches' (one of the many colourful nicknames he used for them) and I knew she would be on tenterhooks when they were together. Normally, she loved entertaining visitors and went out of her way to make them feel welcome. Looking back years later, it was clear to me that she had decided on her tactics in advance. She would make it clear to the Germans that they were here under sufferance. She would tolerate them and just about be civil to them – but only just.

Whereas Mama was inclined to be too trusting, Papa was more of a realist. He knew that German soldiers billeted in houses were not averse to removing valuable pieces of property that caught their eye. Papa inevitably feared that the two staying with us would be the worst examples of Teutonic manhood. So, we all moved into the sitting room and did a quick mental inventory of items that might be of value as well as sentimental keepsakes. Not surprisingly, as money was now tight in our household, there was little we thought might be of interest. Nevertheless, there was an old carriage clock that had been in the family for several generations, two silver candlesticks, a porcelain vase and a faded photograph that resided on top of the piano that were selected to be removed for hiding. The photograph of Uncles Maurice and Benoit in their uniforms and sporting enormous moustaches taken before giving their lives for France in the Great War had always meant a lot to Papa.

Then we remembered Mama's jewellery and furs, handed down from her mother and probably further back than that. Now they were valuable! She also remembered Papa's old hunting rifle which had not been used for years. Apparently, he was keeping it for me when I was old enough.

Possession of any firearms by any member of the local population was punishable by death according to what Mama had read. Papa said he had the perfect hiding place. It was somewhere I had heard about but not actually seen myself.

Under the heavy dresser in the kitchen, there was a small, enclosed space. Our house was at least a hundred and fifty years old and during that time there had been many border disputes and periods of lawlessness. The village had been raided on several occasions and many of the occupants had taken precautions to establish places where valuables could be secreted. In our case, the then owner had dug out a space beneath the cellar floor and cleverly concealed the entrance. Over the years, the cellar had become the kitchen, but the cubby hole had been retained. During our ownership, a substantial piece of furniture now stood on top of it.

It took several attempts to prize open the trap door but finally, with our helper Monsieur Mercier, it gave way. The first thing I was aware of was the smell of fustiness and decay and as Mama shone her torch into the space, I saw insects scurrying across the rubble floor to the corners to avoid the light. If you could imagine three coffins laid out in a compact row, it would give you the dimensions of the hole. The items designated to be of value, together with the hunting rifle, were placed carefully on hessian sacks in the hole and then the kitchen was restored to its normal state.

In the middle of the afternoon of the following day, the moment we had all been dreading finally arrived. A staff car and a motorbike arrived simultaneously. There was a rap at the door. Esmé, our golden retriever, immediately started barking. I quickly took her by the collar and ushered her away. Mama had gone to open the door. I peered sheepishly through the window. Two men stood there in field grey uniforms. The younger of the two took off his cap and said in faltering French. 'Madame Rolland, I understand you have been expecting us. My name is Leutnant Emmerich and this is Major Albrecht.' Two pairs of heels clicked in unison.

Supper that night was a quiet, almost formal affair. Papa staggered into the dining room on his crutches and said a very gruff hello. Either the light had caught his gold filing or else he had deliberately polished it, nonetheless it was very bright and gave him rather a piratical appearance. Much to Mama's relief and mine, he decided to eat his food elsewhere. In his own way he was making his point.

It was clear that the senior officer of the two, Major Albrecht, spoke no French at all. There was certainly nothing wrong with his appetite as he tucked heartily into the uncharacteristically thin rabbit stew that Mama had produced. He appeared not to be totally bereft of manners and muttered a few words of appreciation of Mama's cooking which were duly translated by the other man. Albrecht was a large, broad-shouldered man of about forty years of age. He had a weather-beaten face, close cropped blond hair and exuded strength and menace. The latter was exacerbated by what looked like a duelling scar that ran all the way down from his right eyebrow down to his jawbone. Not a man to take liberties with, I thought to myself.

The younger of the two, Leutnant Emmerich, was probably in his early twenties. Tall and rather gangly, he was not your idea of a soldier who would strike fear in your heart. The complete antithesis of the major, he was awkward, nervy and seemed uncomfortable in his superior's presence. So much so, that as he reached for the salt, he knocked his glass of wine all over Mama's freshly laundered white tablecloth. He spoke some French and managed, poor man, to stammer out an apology for the spillage. Strangely, he seemed more confident exchanging a few pleasantries with us than conversing with the major until the latter gave him a glare which shut him up. The rest of the meal was conducted in silence except for the growling of Esmé who had to be removed from the room. Finally, he translated the major's instruction that they were now going to retire upstairs. I stifled a laugh as he made it sound like they were going to bed together.

I helped Mama with the washing up afterwards. We both agreed that we could have done a lot worse with our two Germans. Albrecht was clearly not a man to be trifled with, but the lieutenant seemed shy, sensitive – almost human. Mama asked me whether I had noticed his beautiful hands, his long and delicate fingers. When we told Papa about this, he said that the only good German was a dead one.

The same routine lasted for about three or four days. The two men would arrive back from their duties early evening. They would clean themselves up, join us for a monosyllabic meal and retire soon afterwards. On each of these occasions, the usually friendly Esmé would growl at the first sight of the two Germans and had to be relegated to spend supper with Papa.

Then we didn't see them for four days. When they did finally appear one evening, they were dishevelled and exhausted. They went straight to bed and slept for twelve hours or so. During this time, Papa had several visitors. He became quite animated for him. It was clear that something was up.

War had finally come to our little corner of the mountains. One of Papa's visitors knew Frenchmen who lived locally and who were part of a resistance group that were helping the British. I learned that only the other day one of them had lit fires to act as beacons to guide aircraft to a prepared drop zone. They had watched the paratroopers descend from the sky and had helped them carry parachuted containers of weapons, ammunition and food to hiding places in the forests. To this day, I still remember the exact words that Papa used. 'All hell is about to be let loose.'

As a ten-year-old boy, I knew enough to know that our peaceful existence was about to be disrupted, but the prospect of guns and battles (which I might see with my own eyes!) had me up all night. Unsurprisingly, I was full of this when I went that afternoon to a school friend's house to play. Aurélien knew as much as I did but he added to my anticipation when he told me that he had heard gunfire and explosions some distance away during the night. He also had two German soldiers billeted in his house, as had other school friends. We discussed what our respective lodgers were like. We decided it was good news that the Resistance was helping the British and their knowledge of the forest tracks would enable them to keep one step ahead of the Germans. It was a game of cat and mouse. The big question was how long would it be before the Americans arrived and we would be liberated?

The major wasn't at supper that night, so we had Leutnant Emmerich or Günther, as he insisted we call him, to ourselves for the evening. Esmé was as good as gold during the evening and occupied her normal place under the table hoping that the occasional scrap would find its way on to the floor. The subject of Adolf Hitler and the state of the war was sadly off limits, but he did let slip that there was 'a lot going on' in the area now. Mama had made a bit more of an effort with supper. As he tucked into a plateful of her hearty cassoulet and a glass or two of red wine, his inhibitions seemed to vanish and without the major there, he became quite effusive.

The alcohol seemed to liberate his knowledge of the French language too because we understood a fair amount of what he said. He was twenty-three years old and came from the beautiful and ancient city of Heidelberg. He was the youngest of three brothers. He became quite emotional when he told us that his eldest brother had been killed in Russia in 1941. The middle one was in the submarine service and at sea somewhere. His father had been a manager of a factory that produced paper. With one of their sons dead, both parents lived in constant fear of hearing bad news about the other boys.

With Papa in his bedroom and Mama constantly on her feet bringing food or clearing plates, most of Günther's conversation seemed to be directed at me. Several customers who bought paper from his father's factory had been French which meant that he had spent time in France after the Great War. Günter said he had French cousins and had visited them quite often which explained how he had a smattering of French. Those visits had been happy occasions and mostly in summer. He remembered picnics, camping trips and fishing in the lakes. I told him I was a boy scout, and we had an annual camping expedition during which, amongst many other activities, I had learnt to fish.

Mama re-joined us after a while and poured herself another glass of wine. Günther asked her about the piano he had spotted in the sitting room. Was it in tune? He asked. She replied she thought so. Would she mind if he had a go? The three of us moved into the sitting room. Günther played and we listened. Although I do not have an ear for music, I could tell from the unfaltering way he played and how he almost tickled the notes, all without the need for music, that he was a talented pianist. The entire time Mama sat engrossed, enthralled even by his sweet tones. When he'd finished, we gave him a little round of applause as he closed the top and slipped self-consciously off to bed.

It was clear that during the one and a half hours we

were together, Günther forgot about the war and became wrapped up in telling us about his childhood and piano playing. Mama and I both agreed that Günther's skills had transported us away from the troubles of the moment also. She added that while he was a German loyal to his country, Günther was certainly not a Nazi.

The next day, 10th September 1944, our world turned upside down.

It all started the next morning when Aurélien and I were in the small village square on our bikes. We were just debating which of the two cafés was going to get our custom for a drink and a snack when Monsieur Michel, our deputy mayor, appeared and beckoned me over to talk to him. He was a small man and looked rather flustered as he asked, 'Is your mother at home?'

'Yes,' I said. 'She was hanging out the washing when I left.'

'What about the Germans?' he enquired further.

'They left early this morning at their usual time.' I replied.

'Thank goodness. I need to speak to her urgently. You'd better come too. You may be needed.'

I called across at Aurélien and told him I had to go. I accompanied Monsieur Michel the short distance to our house. The Deputy Mayor was not a regular visitor to the house, so I was curious to find out what was afoot. I lent my bike up against the fence, strode through the open front door and called out for Mama. She came out from Papa's room immediately and on seeing our visitor flashed one of her famous smiles.

'Monsieur Michel, how lovely to see you. What can I do for you?' I looked at him. His face was very serious. No time for pleasantries, I thought.

'Thank you, Madame Le Rolland. Events necessitate that I speak to you and your husband as a matter of the utmost importance and secrecy. I understand the German officers are not here now. Is there somewhere we can talk in privacy? As your husband is incapacitated, I think it is as well your son is present because his assistance may be required.' As usual I could only understand about a third of what he was saying. But needless to say, I was intrigued.

By now, curiosity had given way to desperation to find out what was going on. Mama took us to the bedroom where Papa was sitting in the armchair with his foot on a stool reading an old newspaper. Mama explained to him that Monsieur Michel had something important to tell us. The Deputy Mayor cleared his throat, drew himself up to his full height (which wasn't very high), took a deep breath and began in his rather self-important fashion.

'Madame Le Rolland, I have come to you because you are a trained nurse. You are no doubt cognisant of the fact that the Germans have brought in specialist troops into our villages and woods and are on the hunt for British parachutists who were dropped a few nights ago.' Papa started muttering to himself again at the mention of the German soldiers.

'Shush, Freddy. Let Monsieur Michel continue.' Mama interjected.

'As I was saying, about the British parachutists. Last night there had been a full moon and it was particularly luminous. I found it difficult to sleep. I was awake early and decided to take the dog out in the woods. A few minutes later, I heard someone behind me say 'Monsieur.' There stood a man in battledress I didn't recognise. He told me he was a British soldier.' The Deputy Mayor cleared his throat again. A British soldier in OUR village several hundred metres from here. Wow! I thought to myself. He carried on.

'He told me that he and his companion had been involved in an exchange of fire with a German patrol the day before yesterday. They had managed to escape but his companion had been shot in the arm. They had been hiding up in the woods, but the wound had deteriorated and now required urgent medical attention.'

Monsieur Michel was by now beginning to perspire. He took his handkerchief out and mopped his brow. 'You can imagine, Madame Le Rolland, I was a little taken aback by this.'

'Perfectly understandable, Monsieur,' Mama replied. I could tell she knew where this was going.

'I told the Englishman that I needed a moment to ponder. In our little village, the only person I could think of who was medically trained was you, Madame. After a short while, I told him that I was a man of some status locally and that I had to think of my position. However, I did know of somebody who might be able to assist, and I would do what I could.'

Monsieur Michel stopped talking and looked at us, now using the handkerchief to dab the corners of his mouth. He hadn't reckoned on this when he put himself forward for Deputy Mayor, I thought. For a while, nobody spoke. I guessed that my parents' brains were going at full speed weighing up the implications, risks and logistics of the step that our family might possibly be about to take. While Mama, Papa and even I knew only too well that the penalty was death for aiding and abetting the enemy and how ruthless the Germans were, my ten-year-old thoughts were all about the thrills and adventures that it might bring. Mama, of course, was the first to speak. Once a nurse, always a nurse.

'I'll go and get my medical bag'.

Then Papa entered the fray. Predictably he was keen to put one over the old enemy. However, he urged more thought before Mama went roaring off to provide help. His brain had not been idle, and several things had occurred to him. First, would this just be a case of going to the aid of an injured man or would it escalate into helping the enemy of our occupier? We all know the punishment for that, don't we? A public execution, most likely a hanging to deter others. Secondly, while he was desperate to do anything to damage the grey lice, his gammy leg would prevent him from taking any active part himself. The likely fallout from this would be that I would have to step up to assist Mama. Was it right that I, their ten-year-old son and only child, should be involved in something as dangerous as this? Thirdly, in case we had forgotten, we did have two German officers – or Boche bastards, as he put it, staying with us. However, we might only be talking about a few days because liberation was at hand.

Mama said that Papa was right but that this was a conversation to be had further down the line. We were getting ahead of ourselves as we were not sure at this stage what we would be dealing with. Her first duty was to help a badly wounded man and once she had attended him and made her assessment, we would be in a better position to judge what we might be letting ourselves in for.

Mama left a short while later with Monsieur Michel clutching her hastily assembled medical bag. They had agreed beforehand to walk on separate sides of the street so as not to arouse suspicion. She was gone a couple of hours during which time I had been pacing up and down and chattering nervously at Papa who responded with an occasional grunt.

Mama returned. The journey through the village had been uneventful and as they had approached the soldiers' hideout, Monsieur Michel had whistled. Years later after Mama had died, I found her diaries at the bottom of a box in the loft. In the 1944 one, she described her initial impressions of the two Englishmen.

'The first of them I see is a tall, strong, handsome young man of about thirty with several days' beard growth. This does not spoil the charming manner with which he greets me. I immediately see he is the one who is not hurt. He speaks good French and takes me to his friend who is lying on a blanket.'

Mama lit an extremely rare cigarette. The wounded man was called Denis and they were both officers: Denis, a major and Andy, a captain. The bad news was that a bullet had made a mess of Denis's forearm and the early stages of gangrene were evident. The correct medicine was needed urgently, and it was likely that she may have to amputate his arm. They were also in need of food and drink, having existed for the last few days on grass and wild apples. Mama wrote on a piece of paper a list of the medicine needed and told me to get my bicycle out and ride like the wind over to Bertrichamps, a few kilometres away and show it to the man who ran the pharmacy there. I was not to say for whom the medicine was or what it was for and to return with it as soon as possible.

It seemed we now had the answer to Papa's questions and the die was cast.

I took the flattest route to Bertrichamps which meant I shared the same road as the Germans used for their supplies. There was a steady stream of military traffic heading west. Things were hotting up. It was by now mid-afternoon when I returned with the medication after an uneventful trip. Mama was getting agitated about whether she would have enough time to visit the two British soldiers before the arrival of Major Albrecht and Günter for supper. As ever, she was organised. When I'd been out on my bike, she had prepared the evening meal and assembled some food to take to the British.

'Xavi, I need you to come with me. I can't manage the box of food and my medical bag by myself' she said.

Naturally, I was excited by the prospect of meeting two British soldiers on active service and hoped I might learn something of their mission. However, more important at that moment was to prove to Mama that I was worthy of her trust.

'Of course, Mama.' I replied trying desperately to conceal the excitement coursing through me.

'Good. We must be careful not to draw attention to ourselves and have a story ready if we are stopped.' She said firmly. We discussed this with Papa and together we came up with what we thought was a plausible reason for why we were carrying a medical bag and a box of food. He begged us to be careful.

We set off straight away. My stomach was a bit tight, and my heart was beating faster than normal. During the first few hundred metres, I kept glancing furtively to my left, right and behind me. Mama reprimanded me and told me to act normally. This was not easy, especially as two German soldiers were walking towards us on the same side of the road. I swallowed hard. Mama came to the rescue and told me to look at her while she started talking to me for about the time it takes to boil a potato. The Germans never broke stride. They were chattering away to each other and barely noticed us. I let out a deep breath and started to relax.

We walked on for another fifteen minutes or so through the village and beyond. We then turned on to a minor road and after a short while on to a forest track. The woods at first were quite open but then thickened as younger and smaller trees made the going more difficult. Finally, Mama stopped and began to whistle. Shortly afterwards, a tall, whiskery and scruffily dressed man walked out from behind some saplings. His grubby face had a huge grin on it, as he recognised Mama.

'Madame, it is wonderful to see you. Who have we here?' he said brightly.

'This is my son, Xavier. My husband had a serious accident some years ago and cannot walk. So, I asked Xavi to help me. Not that he needed much persuasion, he was desperate to come.' Mama replied.

I shook hands with the Englishman. 'Does your name begin with an X?' I nodded. 'First time I've ever met somebody whose name starts with an X. My name is Andy – from the other end of the alphabet.' He added – and that's how it began.

Mama was impatient to get on. We followed Andy past some more spindly saplings into a small clearing which itself was almost totally screened off by young trees, at the most three metres high. Andy had found himself an excellent hiding place. There was a large rucksack on the ground with much of its contents strewn around on the earth. To one side, there was a wounded man sitting up against the other rucksack. I saw one of his arms swathed in bandages, some of which were stained with blood and worse. Mama was already leaning over him and removing some of his dressings. His face was grubby too but despite that its pallor was unmistakable. His eyes were sunken, and he looked exhausted. His face grimaced with pain as Mama touched his arm. Andy stood over him translating the conversation between the wounded man and Mama. My eyes strayed to the two submachine guns lying nearby ready for instant use.

After a few minutes, Mama stood up and I saw the man prop himself up on his good arm and smile at me. His voice was weak, and he told me in halting French that his name was Denis but that everyone called him Denny and that my mother was a saint and he felt better already. I think that was bravado talking as I heard Mama saying to Andy that Denny might lose his arm. He needed his dressings changed regularly, food, warmth, lots of sleep and a few prayers from the rest of us if it was to be saved. Denny then sank back on to the rucksack as though that short exchange of words had consumed the last of his strength.

Mama then took the lid off the box and produced with a flourish: bread, a hunk of cheese, some sliced saucisson, a small tarte aux pommes, a bottle of water and one of red wine. I could tell the men were desperately hungry. Andy tore off some bread and cheese and poured some water into a glass. He then went over to Denny, gently lifted his head and cradled it gently in the crook of his arm. He then brought the glass up to Denny's lips, tilted it while his comrade gulped it down. Andy then broke the bread into smaller pieces which Denny made short work of. Only then did Andy feed himself.

Whist I was watching this surprising moment, Mama had packed up her medical bag and put the lid on the food box. She was in a hurry to get back so we said our farewells and told them we would return tomorrow to check on Denny's condition and bring some food. Meanwhile they were to stay safe. Andy expressed his gratitude for the medical help and food. He was also aware of the risks they were taking.

'See you tomorrow, Xavi,' he said and gave me a wink.

We set off in silence and it wasn't until we had got to the edge of the village that I suddenly turned to Mama and whispered. 'Did you see those guns?'

'My darling Xavi', she replied. 'I love you with all my heart. But if you think you're getting within fifteen metres of a gun then you're a bigger fool than old Madame Noirtier next door.'

We briefed Papa on how the visit had gone. Mama said she had been thinking on the way back that it would be a lot more convenient if the Englishmen could be hidden closer to our house. Denny's arm would need regular care if it was to be saved which could take several weeks. Daily trips with a medical bag and large food box would inevitably arouse suspicion. Papa paused for a while. We all realised that this was a pivotal moment which ultimately might make the difference between life and death. In decisions of this nature, Mama would defer to Papa. In the end the decision was easy. Papa looked at Mama quizzically. Mama nodded once immediately and assertively, then Papa looked at me and I did the same. At Mama's behest, we put our hands together and asked God for his support in what we were about to do. It was the first time in years I had heard Papa mutter 'Amen'.

Just at that moment, we heard the familiar sound of the motor bike and staff car. We now had to switch our concentration on to the Germans and not give anything away about our double- or was it now treble- life?

The two Germans, punctual as ever, arrived just as the food was being brought to the table. The major was clearly dog tired and made short work of the plateful that Mama put in front of him. He grunted a few words which could have been thanks and disappeared upstairs. Günther stayed a while longer, so I poured him a glass of wine. He told us a little more about his childhood in Heidelberg and how his family had kept a small sailing boat on the Neckar. Having expressed his thanks for yet another delicious dinner, he got up to leave the table. He then paused a while before walking to the door to the hall, which he opened carefully. He went into the corridor but a moment later returned to the kitchen closing the door as quietly as he could. He looked anxious and said in a low voice.

'Madame, I urge you to be very careful over the next few days. Stay in the house as much as you can.' With a click of the heels, he was gone.

Mama and I looked at each other. Was it a general warning or was it aimed at us specifically? We told Papa about it and together we decided that to the best of our knowledge the Germans had nothing to connect us to any British parachutists, if that was what it was all about. However, Papa told us that his friend, Philippe Mercier, had visited earlier in the day. He had heard a lot of gunfire coming from further down the valley. All the signs were that time was not on our side and that we would somehow have to move the two Englishmen to a more secure and accessible location as soon as possible. Papa then appeared to look rather pleased with himself. He beamed – something he didn't do very often. He'd had an idea.

'I've thought of the perfect place to hide our English friends. If we can somehow move them to the caves at Les Roches d'Ortomont up there,' He pointed towards the garden at the back of the house at the end of which the ground rose sharply to yet more thick woods. 'Then you would both be able to come and go as you please without being seen by anybody.'

'Except Albrecht and Emmerich. But it's a great idea, darling.' Mama paused a moment. 'How do we do it?'

Les Roches d'Ortomont would be ideal, I thought; isolated and known only to a few (including some of my school friends – it was a great place to play): a good vantage point from which to see if anybody was approaching: cover from rain, wind and cold: only twenty minutes from our house. Mama was right though, getting them up there would be extremely difficult.

Papa could see that Mama especially and I were exhausted after the day's physical exertions. It seemed like it was days ago that Monsieur Michel had met me in the town square and yet it was only this morning. In that time, Mama had made two visits to attend to a wounded British paratrooper. I had bicycled a considerable distance as fast as I could to pick up some vital medication to save an arm, possibly a life. Mama had cooked supper and entertained, albeit briefly, two German officers. Add to this all the nervous and emotional strain, it was no wonder that we were completely done in.

Thank goodness! We had both slept well even the roar of Günter's motor bike at 6.00am failed to wake me. Papa, on the other hand, had been busy studying a map, marking it in a red pen and jotting down notes. Mind you, he still had a gleam in his eye. This was his moment. He was enjoying it. After breakfast, we gathered in Papa's room for our briefing. He had decided the plan of action. He did not give either of us a chance to speak and was adamant and stern in his assertion that his wife and son were not going to put themselves in danger. It was ludicrous to even think of being involved in moving the two Englishmen through an area that was swarming with the Boches. They would have to do it themselves. We're talking about parachutists who are highly trained in navigation and evasion by day or night, he said. The distance they would have to cover was not far and with the aid of a detailed local map which showed footpaths and forest paths, the two men should be able to accomplish it without much difficulty.

'Do you think they will be able to find the caves themselves, Papa?' I asked.

'Yes,' he replied. 'This is what the paras and other elite soldiers do best. Map reading by night is something they should be able to do in their sleep. Myrhiam, do you think the injured one is fit enough to walk for an hour or so tonight?'

'I'll see how he is this morning. There's nothing wrong with his legs and if I make sure his arm is secure in the sling, he'll probably manage. He certainly won't be able to carry his rucksack though. Andy will have to bring it.'

We set off for the hideout half an hour later. Papa had found the map and pointed out to Mama where les Roches was and where they were now. She had hastily put some food and drink into the box. Thank goodness, our journey was uneventful. We whistled and Andy appeared shortly after. He wasn't grinning this time. Instead, he looked anxious and extremely relieved to see us.

'We've had a bit of excitement, Xavi', was the way he put it. A woman from the village had accidentally stumbled on their camp. Andy wasn't sure whether she was friend or foe but nevertheless had decided it was time to move on. I looked around me. While Denny was still sitting propped up against his rucksack, the place was much tidier. They were getting ready for a speedy departure. Mama hurried over to check on Denny who, even to my untrained eye looked a little perkier and had a marginally better colour. He had apparently had a good night's sleep, presumably the result of having some food inside his stomach and the drowsiness brought on by the medication Mama had given him. She then removed the dressing and inspected the wound. It was cleaner and although the gangrene was still present, it had not deteriorated any further.

'Well done, Denny. We may save that arm yet.' She said as he managed to raise a weak smile. Although he was the senior officer, he was certainly not yet well enough to take the lead. Mama quickly and skilfully redressed the wound.

She turned and addressed Andy. 'We had already decided that it was best for you to move somewhere easier for us to get to you but that woman discovering your camp has clinched it. We think we have found the perfect place for you to hide.' Mama was well into her stride now telling them what was going to happen despite Andy's protestations about the risks they were taking and that she should leave the two Englishmen to fend for themselves.

She was having none of it. 'Denny is not out of danger yet; his arm still needs plenty of care and dressings. He is certainly not well enough to live rough and take his chance with the enemy.' I could see why she became the head nurse at the hospital in Raon l'Étape. She didn't stand any nonsense. They did as they were told. However, her tone was less harsh when she asked whether Denny could walk for an hour and a quarter at the most. If he was unable to, then Papa's plan wouldn't work, and a rethink would be necessary. So, she asked him to stand up.

With Andy's assistance and much effort, he struggled to his feet and took a few faltering steps. He then turned to us and said he would damned well give it a go. If one of us could find him a robust stick which could support his weight and he could turn it into a walking stick, then his chances would be even better. That was my job. As to the other logistical difficulties, Andy would have to carry both rucksacks and submachine guns. As trained paratroopers, they were ready to cope with the unforeseen.

Before launching into the instructions for the evening jaunt, as she called it, Mama wanted reassurance that Andy was confident about finding his way in the pitch dark. While Freddie had said they would be able to, she had her doubts. Calmly and with no sense of bravado, Andy replied that the night's walk was part of their basic training, and he could do it blindfolded even carrying most of Denny's kit.

Reassured, she handed over the map on which Papa had marked the route from their hiding place to our house, avoiding the roads and using obscure forest tracks. She reminded the two men that if they were captured that the map would implicate the Rolland family. To which Andy said we were not to worry because he would make a copy of the route and then bury the map. Mama then went on to explain that this was not their ultimate destination but, for a few hours only, they were to hide in a small wood directly behind the house. She showed them exactly where it was on the map and reminded them that there were two German soldiers in the house.

As far as she was aware, apart from the soldiers billeted in houses in the village, the only concentration of troops was in the castle on the heights overlooking the valley on the other side from their house. At the most, she thought, the distance they would have to cover was a mere four kilometres. She suggested that, in anticipation of the nocturnal jaunt, they should rest up for the remainder of the day, tuck into the food and drink she had brought them. Andy said that they would be mindful of the possibility that the lady who had stumbled upon their camp earlier would have informed the Germans. In which case, there would be a gun battle and that would be it.

Pierre-Percée was a small village, said Mama. She knew most of the residents and was not aware of any who were pro German but, nonetheless, she would pray to God that all would be well. She reminded them that our two Germans left the house around 6.00am. Shortly afterwards, I was to check whether the Englishmen were there and, if so, we would be serving them a real French breakfast with piping hot coffee. How about that for an incentive?

Chapter Two

Supper was a quieter affair than ever that evening, at least until Esmé livened up the proceedings. To start with, the two Germans seemed preoccupied with their thoughts – maybe of home, past battles or what the future might hold. Then Esmé joined us in the dining room. We thought nothing of it as we assumed that she had got used to the uniforms. The growling started from under the table and grew in intensity. Otto looked to see what was happening. This induced a snarl and a snap from Esmé. Otto lashed out with his boot connecting with the poor, unfortunate animal which yelped in pain and responded by launching itself at Otto's leg. There then followed an outburst of pain and rage from Otto. Apparently, Esmé had embedded her teeth into his lower thigh. This was a dog that had never snarled or snapped in its life and certainly never bitten anyone. Mama leapt to her feet and grabbed Esmé by the scruff of her neck and dragged her into Papa's room.

On her return, she saw that the German had removed his boot and rolled up his trouser leg to inspect the damage. Two shallow teeth marks were evident which had barely broken the skin but there was a little blood. Mama retrieved her medical bag and administered some anti-septic, all the while muttering her apologies 'Entschuldigung, Entschuldigung, Herr Major.' The most flustered participant in all of this was Günther whose job it was to translate a tirade from a very angry Otto. The major had said that if that f…dog ever so much as growled at him again he would shoot it dead on the spot.

The major then spoke gruffly to Günther again. They would not be needing supper the next night as 'something had come up'. Mama and I exchanged a quick glance. This was nothing to do with the dog bite. It was a very difficult game we were playing, so any remark like that was going to cause us anxiety. Meanwhile, Papa was grinning from ear to ear and, as he had been fondling Esmé on his lap was saying to her what a clever girl she was.

September 13th dawned with a chill in the air and low cloud over the mountains and forests. I heard the Germans leave at first light and did a quick check of their rooms which revealed that they had taken most of their kit with them. I dressed quickly and went downstairs where Mama was already busy in the kitchen. I could see from her face she had had a bad night. True to her word, she was making coffee for our English friends. Even to me the smell of it was very appetising and the only time I had ever taken a sip I'd spat it out.

Of course, the burning question was had Andy and

Denny made it safely to the spinney behind the house? Papa asked me to go to the edge of it and whistle to see if there was any response. He didn't want fresh hot coffee wasted if they weren't there.

The big moment had arrived. I could feel a tremor of excitement (or was it apprehension?) in me as I opened the back door. I went through the gate at the end of the garden and made my way up the slope into the bracken to a small group of fir trees which we called 'The Spinney'. My mouth was dry and my first attempt at a whistle was feeble, so I took a deep breath to give it another go. I know now that there was a pair of eyes watching me because then I heard Andy's voice calling out softly.

'Morning, Xavi. Denny and I would give our right arm for some of your mum's coffee.' Denny laughed and mumbled something, which Andy then translated for my benefit: he wouldn't mind keeping at least one, thank you very much.

They had made a snug little hiding place for themselves. Their night jaunt was uneventful, although understandably Denny had found the going tough. They had arrived about three hours before and had rested up. Andy asked what the plan was.

I relayed Papa's instructions, but it was breakfast that was at the forefront of their minds. When I got back inside, Mama had been watching from the kitchen window and was already frying eggs to take up on two trays with slices of ham and bread and butter. A short while later, we carried them out to the two Englishmen who were by now sitting up against their backpacks.

Unsurprisingly, they made short work of what was on their plates, murmuring barely intelligible thank-yous as they shovelled the food down. Mama then turned her attention to Denny's arm. Careful and methodical as she was, Denny still winced and breathed in sharply. She pronounced herself satisfied that the gangrene had stabilised, and things would begin to slowly get better from now on, providing Denny was a good boy and did as he was told. However, plenty of rest would still be necessary. She told them in a few hours 'her boys', as she called them from now on, would have to move up the steep slope to two caves that overlooked the valley. The journey would normally take twenty minutes but with a wounded man it would be longer. It should be the ideal hiding place, she said. Only a few locals know of its existence and something else in its favour, it was an excellent vantage point from which to spot anybody's approach.

Mama then posed an unusual question to the two men. If they could be granted a wish at that moment, what would it be? Andy mumbled something about a dinner with the prettiest girl in the Vosges for company. Denny said a good night's sleep in a warm bed.

'Might a hot bath be on your list?', she said with a grin. 'With the greatest respect, you smell a little, let's say ripe. It's a perfect opportunity to have a soak in the tub while our German house guests are away.' It was a popular suggestion, and a happy procession that entered the house that morning.

In all the drama of the last few days, I had quite forgotten that Papa had not yet met them. Papa was unusually jovial, and we had an exchange of 'Vive la France' followed by 'Vive l'Angleterre' and plenty of backslapping. Andy was complimented on his command of French and his accent. When Denny was asked about his ability in the language, he rather formally said how pleased he was to meet everybody and could we point him to the nearest library. His face then broke into a smile and then uttered 'voilà' accompanied by a typical Gallic gesture. Clearly that was as far as his French went. Then Esmé came lolloping up to them, wagging her tail furiously. Both men were pleased to see her but Denny doubly so. It was the first time I'd seen his smile reach his eyes as he patted her with his good arm and rubbed his nose against hers. 'Just like my Tinker', he said with a laugh.

Papa asked Denny for a few details of their operation and how he came to be wounded. With Andy interpreting, he said liberation for France was at hand and the Americans could be here any day now. He didn't give away much about their part in the proceedings, only that he and Andy were in a large group on the way to a rendezvous when they were ambushed. In the chaos of the firefight, he took one in the arm and the two of them became separated from their comrades. He added finally and most poignantly that he owed his life to his comrade and friend, a claim Andy instantly dismissed.

Mama obviously thought that this little exchange of bonhomie had gone on far too long and there were things to be done. I was despatched a short way along the lane to act as lookout in case of surprise visitors during bath time. Half an hour later, I was summoned back to the house and was greeted by a clean and shaven Andy who asked me what time we had to leave to get to the Savoy in time for our reservation.

He and Denny were keen to move to their new hiding place as it was obviously risky to linger in the house longer than necessary. Mama and Papa had been discussing the immediate requirements for their stay in the caves: blankets, cushions, candles and a small stove, rations of bread, apples and water. Once they settled in, there would no doubt be other requirements. Papa would dearly love to help, he said, but because of his accursed leg it was not possible.

After Papa finished, Andy delivered a little speech. He praised the Rolland family's bravery, their kindness, and Mama's exceptional nursing and cooking skills. At one point he seemed to channel Churchill, emphasising the historical links that bind our nations together (I decided it wasn't the moment to mention Agincourt and Waterloo). He expressed their deep gratitude for our help but stressed that they were determined not to keep us in danger any longer than necessary. They intended to move on as soon as possible, First and foremost, he and Denny were trained soldiers, and they had an important job to do. In a matter of days when the wound had healed, they would re-join their comrades and continue the fight.

The formalities over, it was now time to make a move. Denny was clearly in no fit state to make the stiff climb up to the caves. Andy reckoned he could carry him with a few stops along the way. It would take several trips to bring the guns, the rucksacks and rations up to the caves. So, taking great care to avoid any contact with his wounded left arm, Andy hoisted Denny over his shoulder and off we set to their new home on the side of a hill, Mama leading with me bringing up the rear.

The early mist was long gone as we followed a distinct path through the trees for some of the way, pausing every couple of minutes to give Andy a break. After about a quarter of an hour, we left the path where the woods thinned out and started clambering over loose rocks and low scrub. Difficult terrain for Andy but he was heartened by Mama who told him we were almost there. Mama proposed leaving Denny briefly while she guided Andy to the challenging path leading to the caves. We came across a few rock formations that fooled Andy into believing he had reached his destination. However, a short while later, we reached a clearing in the trees, revealing a breathtaking view of the valley. Our village nestled amidst the forested hills on the opposite side, and familiar as I was with it, I couldn't help but be awestruck by the vista.

'It's beautiful.' As he uttered those words, he had no idea that he was standing on the roof of one of the caves that was about to become their home.

He glanced down at me, his face breaking into a smile. 'Well, Xavi, here's the deal. The not-so-great news is that we might be stuck here for a while. Denny's got a jolly nasty injury, and it'll take some time for him to get back on his feet. So, if your mother can spare you, it would be fantastic to have you around for some company now and then. These caves are something else. I can imagine you having fun here during the school holidays.' Andy's smile reassured me, and I knew spending time with this guy wouldn't be a chore.

We moved into our house right before I was born. Not long after settling in, Mama and Papa were out exploring the area, getting acquainted with the surroundings, when they stumbled upon the caves by sheer chance. They asked around the village about them, but only a handful of people were aware of their existence.

'Look at this cave,' I pointed to the nearest one along our route. 'The Germans widened and squared its entrance during the First World War. It served as a store, I believe.' With that, Andy and I crossed the threshold. It was about five or six paces deep and roughly five feet high. Andy, being tall, had to stoop, while I could stand comfortably. There was another cave next to it, untouched by the Germans. Its entrance was narrow, and we had to crawl on all fours to enter. It was deeper than the first one, and when we emerged, Andy clapped his hands in excitement. 'Excellent. It's the Ritz of rock cavities,' he said, pointing at the one with the small opening. 'This can be our dormitory, and the one next door can be our sitting room. I could look at that view forever.' I refrained from mentioning that the weather in the mountains would deteriorate in a couple of weeks with the arrival of autumn.

Andy then went to retrieve Dennis. He managed to bring him up the last few difficult yards with Mama telling him where to put his feet. There was a lot of grunting and groaning from the pair of them as they struggled up the final series of twisty paths through the rocky outcrops. Then with a huge sigh of relief, Denny had arrived at his new home.

While Mama checked his wound, Andy came and re-joined me on the top of one of the caves. I remembered that he had asked me about the holidays, so I told him that I had brought some of my school friends up here and 'mucked about'. We spent one night up here in the spring. 'It was a little spooky', I conceded.

Andy who was about to spend the first of many nights up here, said 'Spooky? Interesting. Do you think the caves are haunted and are full of ghosts?' He pronounced the word 'ghosts' in a tremulous manner to add effect. We both laughed.

'Once when I was about your age and at boarding school, I had to spend a couple of hours in an old graveyard as a dare. It was the last thing I wanted to do as deep down I'm a bit of a coward when it comes to ghosts and ghouls. But as you'll know, you can't back down from a dare or you'll never hear the end of it. Sure enough it was terrifying, with owls hooting up in the yew trees and a full moon throwing shadows everywhere. Right after the clock struck one, I thought I saw an old woman dressed like a maid from the last century scurry between the gravestones. Before you could say Queen Victoria, I was up over the wall sprinting back to school. So let's hope the only company we have in these caves is the odd woodlouse, eh?'

Andy then asked me about my life in the village. I told him it was small and, on the whole. the folk were friendly. I had outgrown the local school and would be starting at a larger school in Celles in the neighbouring valley. I had a couple of good pals who would be joining me there.

He asked about my friends. I had two very close friends, Aurélien and Maxence. Whether it was riding bicycles, exploring the woods, or going fishing, Aurélien and I were inseparable. Maxence was actually my cousin, and along with his sister Elodie, lived with my uncle Gérard and aunt Camille in Moussey. I often visited their place so we could play.

Andy smiled as Mama came to join us having finished dressing Denny's wound. The latter was understandably exhausted by the house move (as Andy put it) and needed plenty of rest. He told Mama what we had been talking about and said if you like mountains, fresh air and having few people around you, you live in a wonderful part of the world. Mama asked him about where he lived.

Andy chuckled. 'It couldn't be more different to the mountains where you are. I live on the edge of the cliff in the middle of the south coast of England. My father is a headmaster of a school about four hundred metres from the sea.' I couldn't believe it. I had never seen the sea and thought this sounded like something from a storybook.

'Like you with the forests and mountains here, it was an idyllic place to grow up. I have two brothers, and during the holidays, we'd build dens in the school's thirty acres. Heaven, really. We'd chase each other on our bikes, kick footballs around, and collect butterflies in the woods. And if we wanted, we'd just cut through a farmer's field and be down on the beach.'

'Mon Dieu, I would be sunbathing every day,' my mother replied.

'Well, yes, although this is England we're talking about.' said Andy. 'The weather down there was more likely to be wild and windy. At night in the middle of a gale, I often lay awake in bed hearing the waves crashing against the shore, pulled the bedclothes around me and thought, 'God help sailors on a night like this.'

He was very talkative for someone we barely knew.

Mama wanted to know how come Andy spoke such immaculate French.

'I'm lucky enough to have an ear for languages.' Before the war started, he explained that he had been working for an oil company which involved a lot of travel to France. We learned later that one of the reasons he had been selected for this mission was his excellent French. In fact, he was an important member of the team, his role being the operational commander's adjutant, his assistant in the field, if you like. His main job was communication; by radio as well as by word of mouth, which included members of the local maquis. The commander would have to be relying on somebody else for that job now because Andy wouldn't be much use separated from the main force without a radio and hiding in a remote cave.

'On the subject of languages, how's your English?' he asked of Mama and me. Mama replied 'A leetel, I am never in England, but I learn a few medical words when I train to be a nurse.' She went on in her own language, 'so any conversations between Dennis and me will have to involve you.' Andy looked at me.

'No. I don't speak eenglish. I learn it at my new school. I do know 'Mr Churchill smoke cigars' and 'How much is that doggy in the window, the one with the waggerly tail.' I looked up, rather embarrassed at my random offerings, especially as I had attempted to sing the last one. 'Well, it's a start,' laughed Andy.

That was the first of the many twice daily visits up to the hideout that I made over the next seven weeks, many of which Esmé joined me on. It seemed she had made a good friend in Denny, whose spirits rose when she appeared. She would rush over to him, wagging her tail furiously and Denny would make a fuss of her. Unless Mama said otherwise, I was never in a particular hurry to get back home. I always took up their breakfast and we chatted while they tucked in. Mama usually checked Denny's dressings at this time. Five or so hours later, I brought their main meal of the day which meant more chat. It was on one of these occasions that Andy asked me about Papa's disability.

Papa and Uncle Gérard ran a sawmill and woodcutting business together near Moussey. One day, Papa was standing in for one of the power-saw operators who was ill. He was sitting at the end of the machine where he should have been when suddenly a large pile of poorly stacked logs collapsed on him. A freak accident. He was lucky to survive, but his right leg had been badly crushed. It was touch and go whether it needed amputation. Finally, they managed to save the leg, but it was useless. He would be confined to crutches and a wheelchair for the rest of his life. I was six years old at the time and so just about old enough to be aware of the changes to our daily lives that the accident brought about.

Worse still was the head injury. The most serious effect of this blow was that it made him unpredictable, moody and, to be honest, difficult to live with. Mama was a saint and took it in her stride. However, I had to confess to finding it difficult. The kind, spontaneous father to whose daily return from work I looked forward so much was no more. Instead, now I rather avoided him, if possible, because all I got otherwise was an undeserved flea in my ear.

The accident and the fact that he would not be able to work had other ramifications too. It was lucky in a way that Uncle Gérard had been able to buy his side of the business. It was also the main reason that I had not enjoyed school. We live in a small village, and everybody knows everybody else and their business.

Two boys in my class had been particularly unpleasant, telling others how my father was a 'cripple'. The next day before lessons had started, one of the boys had hopped past me on one leg, I felt so angry and that I was about to launch myself at the boy and try to beat him into a pulp. We were just squaring up to each other when the teacher came in. The bullies had seen that I wasn't going to be a pushover. That knocked it on the head for a while. However, just towards the end of term, one of them said to me sarcastically, 'it must be fun playing football with your father. Do you use him as a goal post?'

That did it. I went for them both. The three of us rolled around on the floor and grappled for a while. Then we broke apart. Fists flew and elbows administered winding blows to the stomach. Outnumbered as I was, I managed to land a blow to the side of the head of one of them, but I came off worse. They cornered me, and I felt sick with fear at the beating I was about to get, but then thank goodness, the remainder of the class arrived, followed by the teacher.

The classroom was in a mess and the three of us were panting with the effort, dishevelled and rather bruised. I knew if I snitched on them, it would be worse for me in the long run. So, I told the teacher that we'd had a difference of opinion about something. The teacher had said that he was surprised at me, as I was normally a law-abiding citizen. We were punished by the headmaster. But I knew I'd made proper enemies now, and the whole incident had made me afraid of going back to school.

Andy was looking at me, and I suddenly realised how much I had told him. The man was basically a stranger, yet I had told him the most personal things about myself and my family. I remembered he was a tough soldier who had looked death in the eye and maybe even killed people; he probably thought I was cowardly and pathetic.

He asked me some follow-up questions, but I didn't respond, just looked away. I expected him to make some excuse or change the topic of conversation but instead he shifted towards me. To my surprise, he asked me gently why I wouldn't talk to him about it anymore.

'In England, there's a saying that school days are the best days of your life, but it can be brutal sometimes. I grew up being surrounded by boys of different ages, day and night. We had a sort of culture of silence where what happened between the boys stayed between the boys. It was hard if you didn't fit in. I remember once teasing a boy who was effeminate and liked flowers and wasn't like everyone else. I don't know why I did it but I am still ashamed of myself when I think about it twenty years later. It may sound silly but when the war is over, I'd like to find him and tell him I'm sorry.

'And you're not alone, Xavi. I had a bully of my own for a while', Andy said, placing a pinch of tobacco into one of his cigarette papers. 'His name was Francis Farnsworth. I'm not sure when he decided he had it in for me, but he was cruel and he was clever; he chose his moments carefully, usually waiting until I was alone.

When it started, it was to do with Father. He'd say things like because I was the Whale's son (Father's nickname was the Whale – for obvious reasons) I got a much better deal than the other boys: better food, more tuck – that's what we called sweets – a more comfortable bed, minimal punishments and no canings. I told 'Farny' he was being ridiculous and asked him where he had got his information from. He said all the boys were talking about it. I told him that the Whale had caned me a couple of days ago. "Oh, I know you went inside", he said. "Your papa was probably feeding you tuck while he swished the cane against a cushion."

I was getting confused by the words 'caning' and 'beaten', so I asked Andy to explain.

'There are several ways in which a beating can be administered.' He said rather formally as though he was quoting from a handbook. 'The headmaster has three means or tools for dishing out the punishment: for minor offences worthy of a beating, he would use a slipper, next step up was the unforgiving flat side of a hairbrush and for the most serious breaches of the school rules you received 'six of the best' from a bamboo cane. Now that was painful and could draw blood.'

I was stunned by the brutality of this, and the casual way Andy spoke about it. It sounded like something they would do to soldiers in the age of Napoléon. And these were young boys! I kept quiet as I didn't want Andy to be offended by my reaction, but boy, did it make me grateful for the clips around my ears Papa gave me sometimes. And the fact that I wasn't English. No wonder Mama says they're all so buttoned-up, I thought.

I was still eager to hear about Farnsworth. 'Farnsworth told me to show him my bum to prove I had had the cane and there would be bruising to see. I told him he was bonkers and scarpered at the rate of knots. He was older than me and larger too, but I had the advantage of speed, which I used to good effect in the wide-open spaces of the school grounds. However, running inside the school was against the rules and so inevitably he cornered me several times. He punched me hard in the stomach and winded me. It only got worse after that. Did you have a teddy bear when you were younger, Xavi?'

I nodded, leaving out that I still put him in my bed sometimes.

'I had one too. He was brown with a green bowtie that my mother had bought for me when I was born and had been my constant companion ever since. By the time

I was eleven, I was too old to have him in bed with me, but I kept him in a box under my bed in the dormitory and sometimes, if I felt scared or sad, I checked everyone was asleep and secretly took him out. Even though he was quite tatty by then and had shed a lot of his fur, I always found the smell and the feel of him reassuring.' I smiled at the image of this hardened military man with a teddy bear but then thought about how sad it was for a small boy to feel so alone.

'I was obviously not careful enough. One morning, I went upstairs to the dormitory after breakfast and saw some of the boys laughing in the lavatories, which were in the next room. I went over to see what the joke was and then I saw it. My bear's head floating in the lavatory bowl. Someone had cut it off and ripped out the stuffing, which was scattered all over the floor. They had scribbled two red Xs over his eyes. I was stunned, and just had time to pick out the dripping head of my beloved teddy when one of the teachers rang the bell for line-up. As we filed into the hall, I caught the eye of one of the boys. It was Farnsworth and he was smirking. Slowly, he drew his finger across his throat, before sticking out his lower lip to make a 'sad' face.

I was determined not to blub. Although I felt a terrible loss for my poor bear, rage was pulsing through me. Later I told my elder brother Peter about it. He asked me if I wanted him to give Farnsworth a thumping, but I said no. I had to fight my own battles and would deal with him in my own way.'

Andy licked the paper to seal his cigarette and lit it. He breathed in and then exhaled a cloud of smoke with a satisfied sigh. 'Bring me an extra fried egg for breakfast tomorrow and I'll tell you what happened next', he said with a smile.

I was conscious of the fact that I was probably rather quiet at supper that evening. However, I don't think anybody noticed – we had other things on our mind after Otto informed us that he had recently acquired a shotgun and he would like to use it in the woods to shoot some game. Looking at me, he asked whether I could show him the best places to go. Not ideal, when you have two British parachutists hiding there. I looked at Mama for guidance. She said that Xavi would be delighted to, pointing to the east of where the hideout was.

I had arranged early the next morning to show Otto where he could do his shooting. After the two Germans had departed, I did the breakfast run only because later I was going over to Moussey to spend the afternoon with the Millottes. Mama was with us to dress Denny's wound, so there was no opportunity for a follow-up conversation with Andy. Thank goodness, I thought. I felt shy and didn't want to look him in the eye.

I hopped on to my bicycle and made the strenuous ride through the forest to Moussey. The Millotte family had moved here before Papa and Uncle Gérard had set up their sawmill and as close family, we tended to see a lot of each other. Gérard, Mama's brother, was a great bear of a man but gentle with it. As the owner of a sawmill who employed some of the folk from the village, he was a well-respected local businessman. Aunt Camille was robust too and her hugs felt as though she was squeezing the life out of me. She was the noisy member of the family, mind you their daughter, seven-year-old Elodie, came a close second. My pal, Maxence, was a chip of the old block: tall and reserved with the family but really opened up when he and I were together. Gérard had been acutely aware that the things a son would do with his father were not possible for me. So, at the weekend whenever he was doing something with Maxence, he always tried to include me. He had taught Maxence, Aurélien and me how to fish.

Mama, on one of her recent visits, had told her brother and sister-in-law about Andy and Denny but not the children. So that would not be one of today's topics of conversation. However, Gérard did know of other British parachutists being hidden in and around the village, which had become a hotbed of the resistance.

We sat down to lunch. Everyone knew that British parachutists had been dropped all around us and the Germans had brought in special units to round them up. Apparently, there were now SS troops in Moussey and the situation was getting pretty tense. Camille asked me about our two German house guests and whether it had been possible to glean from them what was going on. She had been amused by the nicknames we had given them. I filled them in on my latest observations regarding obdurate Otto and gangling Günther but said they hadn't given anything away. I also told them about Esmé's aversion to Otto and the biting incident under the dinner table. Gérard roared with laughter, that barrel of a chest shaking up and down. 'What a clever and discerning dog she is.' He said and added 'I bet that Papa of yours approved'.

I spent the afternoon hanging out with Maxence. We wandered around the village, especially near the school, which had been occupied by the Germans. There seemed to be a huge amount of hustle and bustle going on: lorries coming and going, groups of soldiers moving hither and thither.

The next morning, Mama and I took up the boys' breakfast. Esmé came too. In fact, she was now a regular visitor up at the caves even staying the occasional night. In fact, it was no bad thing she was out of the way during supper when Otto was likely to be there. She spent a lot of time with Denny which appeared to brighten his day. While Mama, spent her normal half an hour or so checking Denny and chatting to him before leaving, Andy and I sat together on the cave roof. I told him that the Germans were very active after yesterday in Moussey and that Gérard had said 'something was brewing'.

'Andy' I said. He looked at me, slightly concerned. 'Will you tell me about what happened to Farnsworth?'

He laughed. 'Ah yes, happily!' He collected his thoughts for a moment and then carried on. 'So, I don't know what it's like at your school Xavi, but at mine, games were everything. Every weekend we'd have matches in rugger, cricket or whatever it might be against other schools. The older boys in the top teams were idolised, they were like sporting gods, and you'd sell your soul to be like them. Among the boys, intelligence, artistic talent, it meant nothing: if you were a sportsman, you were a 'good egg'. Conversely, the boys who were tubby, scrawny or couldn't catch a ball were usually frowned upon or considered 'wet'.

Luckily for me, I was in the first camp, but Farnsworth certainly was not. He was tall but he was podgy, ungainly and slow. So that gave me an idea...'

At that, he took off his boot and spitting on the leather, gave it a scrub with a small brush. 'Tell me, do you happen to know if your mother has any boot polish, Xavi?'

'ANDY!' I shouted, knowing fully well that he was winding me up.

'Sorry, what were we talking about?' he said with a wink. 'Oh yes. There was only one sporting occasion in the whole year in which every boy in the school had to take part. It was called Sports Day. It was, if you like, a mini-Olympics which featured running races and relay races in which batons were exchanged.

'The school was divided into four 'houses' of twenty boys each, and it was very tribal. Every race was a highly competitive event between the houses and the pressure to win was immense. The climax of the afternoon was the house relay race in which every boy ran. This ensured that the less sporty boys had at least one chance of taking part. There was a ten-minute gap before the last race, when all the boys who had not yet run rushed inside to change.

'On this occasion, I ran inside too but for another reason. In the changing room, I located where Farnsworth was changing but kept my distance. I had my pal, Mostyn, with me. We waited until Farnsworth was almost totally undressed and, on my signal, Mostyn went forward and distracted him with a question about aircraft, a subject we knew he would happily prattle on about for hours. When his back was turned, I dashed in and gathered up the items of his clothing that I was after. In their place I substituted something that I had carefully sought out the previous day from the acting cupboard.

'Meanwhile, outside on the playing fields, the excitement was building, and a crowd had gathered. Father had used his megaphone to tell everybody that the winner of the Grand Athletics Challenge Cup depended on the outcome of the last race. House leaders were scurrying around making sure they had ten boys at each end of the running track. One of the leaders, a terrifying thirteen-year-old named Hogg who had to shave every morning, reported he was one runner short: Farnsworth. Mostyn said he had seen Farny in the changing room whereupon the leader dashed inside in search of the boy. The latter reappeared shortly with a towel round his waist, looking flustered and anxious.

'The tactics used by the four houses varied. Where do you put your fastest runners? Do you space them evenly in the relay team? Do they go in the middle so you can build up a large lead and hope that the last few can hang on or, more commonly, do you place them all at the end for the crucial final straight? These decisions would have been decided before the race. However, the late arrival of Farnsworth and the threat of disqualification for being one man short disrupted his house's plans. He would be the last to run... Perfect, I thought to myself.

'Father fired the starter pistol, and they were off. The noise level increased dramatically as boys all yelled encouragement for their own house. It was chaotic to start with because spectators had no idea who was in the lead.

The crescendo of noise intensified as there were only a few runners left. Even Matron was screaming.

'Mostyn and I had done our sprints. Our attention shifted to Farnsworth who unbelievably still had his towel around his waist. His house leader shouted at him, 'Get ready! What are you doing, you can't run in that!', and yanked his towel away. The top half of his body was dressed as it should have been. However, his running shorts had been replaced by a pair of large Victorian, white-laced bloomers that had once been my grandmother's. The boy before him crossed the line and handed the baton to Farnsworth in first position in the race. He had a big lead and all he had to do was to run seventy-five metres. His strange apparel would not have mattered because the glory would have been his.

'The poor boy started to run, well more like a fast waddle. It was hard to see from where we were sitting whether he was already in tears. If he wasn't then, he would have been very shortly afterwards as all the spectators realised what was going on. Shouts of encouragement from the spectators for the various patrols were replaced by hysterical laughter and pointing of fingers at the wretched child. It went from bad to worse. He dropped the baton of course, and as he bent over to pick it up, the cord holding up the ancient pair of bloomers around his ample bottom finally gave way. So it was that for the last few metres of the race, his waddle became ever more laboured as he endeavoured to keep the baton in one hand and hold up the white bloomers in the other. Meanwhile, two other runners had overtaken him during those crazy last few metres. He stumbled over the line to third place, his house's dreams of the Athletics Cup in tatters.'

Andy himself had struggled to finish the story as he chuckled about his memories of the event. I too laughed and applauded his abilities as a storyteller.

'Did Farnsworth ever find out it was you?' I asked.

'Of course. Later that afternoon, I bumped into Farny. He was lying low in the library and looking very sheepish. I put my arm around his shoulder, thanked him for providing such entertainment and looking him in the eye said slowly and clearly, 'touch me or my things again and next time you'll be starkers.'

He was still chuckling. 'He was meek as a lamb with me after that. After he left the school, I think he went on to…' Andy stopped suddenly mid-sentence, a strange look on his face. He closed his eyes and then said something to himself in English that I didn't understand. 'Andy?' I spoke. 'What is it?'. He looked in my direction, but it was if he was looking straight through me.

'He died', he said softly. 'Farnsworth. He was killed. In forty-two, in Sicily. I saw his name in the newspaper, how could I forget that?' He spoke again in English, this time angrily and the only word I could understand was 'war'. I didn't need to speak English to know what he was saying.

Farnsworth may have been a horrible boy, but maybe he became a good man. And he probably had a mother and a father who loved him. Our laughter from moments ago forgotten, we sat in silence while Andy stared sadly towards the woods.

**

Mama laid on a treat for us that night. Otto had shot a brace of wild duck several days ago. They had been hanging in one of the sheds and Papa had plucked and gutted them. Mama roasted them in a delicious sauce and Otto made some rare complimentary comments which did not need translating. I was even allowed half a glass of wine.

The next day started off normally enough. Mama had made some duck pâté with the leftovers which her boys enjoyed at lunch. Denny had nodded off in the afternoon sun. Andy and I had just made ourselves comfortable prior to starting our conversation on Papa's moods when Esmé joined us looking rather concerned and started growling. We knew what that usually meant. Sure enough, some movement in the trees about a hundred metres below us caught my eye. I leant across and touched Andy's arm. 'Hush' I said putting my forefinger to my lips and pointed with the other hand down the slope, in the direction of the movement I thought I had seen. Andy started to make a fuss of Esmé to keep her quiet.

There was a man with a gun moving cautiously through the woods. I recognised him immediately. It was Otto. Surprise, surprise. Why was he here so early in the afternoon and not where I told him he could shoot? I whispered to Andy who it was and what he was doing. Andy stubbed out his cigarette as quickly as he could. Meanwhile Otto continued to climb upwards in our direction. My first thought was for Esmé, remembering what the German had said after the biting incident and now he had a shotgun in his hand.

Andy moved quickly scooping Esmé up and took her back to Denny. He told me to go and intercept Otto and think up some story along the lines that he is in the wrong part of the forest for game.

'Somehow, you've got to get him to turn back. I'll scoop our stuff up, grab Denny and the dog and get back to the cave as quietly and quickly as possible. Go NOW. If he won't turn back, SHOUT!'

My heart started to beat faster. I slid off the cave roof and headed off down the slope. I saw Otto about seventy metres away. Thank goodness, he had stopped as something behind him had attracted his attention. Predictably I stepped on a fallen branch which broke with a loud crack. Otto whirled around and raised his shotgun.

I raised my hands and said 'Herr Major, it is me, Xavier.' He scowled, disappointed no doubt that I wasn't a small plump deer. He slowly lowered his gun and laid it gently on the ground. On my way down to confront him, I realised the language barrier might come to my aid. The only way to communicate with him was sign language. I started by pretending to fire a gun up in the air and making shooting noises, at the same time moving my hands repeatedly to the left and right. The purpose of this was to indicate to the major that there was no shooting in that part of the forest. He appeared to understand this but looked displeased and said a word that clearly meant 'Why?' I was in trouble now because I didn't have an answer for that. Even if I had, expressing it in cod-sign language I was using would be totally beyond me. All I could say, rather pathetically, was 'Mama' and pointed in the direction of the house. My plan was for both of us to return to the house and Mama would explain why (and get me out of a hole).

Much to my relief, Otto seemed to accept this and so we trotted back to the house. Mama, thankfully, was in the kitchen and I told her why I had returned with the major without mentioning the cave or her boys. Could she please do some rapid thinking and explain why there should be no shooting in that part of the forest? Bless her! Mama called for Leutnant Emmerich to translate and fed him some cock and bull story that the locals had recently shot almost all the wildlife in that part of the forest, and he would be wasting his time. He accepted this, thank goodness. Mama and I heaved a collective sigh of relief.

During supper that night, Otto asked me, via Günther as interpreter, who the other person I had been with in the woods was. Alarm bells rang as he had given me no earlier indication that he had seen anyone else. Mama once again came to my rescue that it must have been one of the foresters who lived nearby and for whom Papa had asked me to run an errand. Phew! She's very good at this, I thought. Had Mama not been there I would have struggled to find a convincing answer.

Of course, I relayed all this to Andy the next morning. He laughed at my little sign language exchange with Otto, applauded me for my quick thinking (and Mama's) and said it had been rather a close shave.

That afternoon Andy asked me more about my father. Had the moods that I had described been consistently bad ever since his accident? Was there anything that seemed to trigger them? Was it me who was usually their target? Was he grumpy with my mother, with other friends, family, the Merciers or the Millottes for example? I thought about it for a moment. I decided I was not going to hold back and would tell it as it was.

'He's grumpy with everybody. People still come and see him but it's because they should rather than they really want to. Apart from Philippe Mercier who is his oldest friend and they both like to gossip and whinge about everything.' Andy smiled at that.

'He loses his temper with Mama occasionally probably because she is bossy and fusses a lot. But I'm the one he goes for, and I have no idea why. I try to be helpful but all I get in return is him barking at me. Sometimes I really hate him. Sometimes I wish that those logs …' I stopped myself there and pushed that thought right out of my mind.

Andy looked thoughtful. 'This situation your family finds itself in is extremely dangerous, Xavi. If you are all going to come through it, you need to make sure you are all on the same side.'

He went on. 'When I was your age, I thought my father was picking on me and unfairly giving me a hard time. I told you he was my headmaster – well, he also taught me maths and I never had a head for numbers. I knew him to be a kind and amusing man but with me he was always gruff and bad-tempered, and he'd treat the other children with more kindness. When I misbehaved – I haven't always been the paragon of virtue you see before you,' he winked, 'I'd often get a beating when others didn't.'

'It wasn't until a few years later that I realised why. My older brother had been at the school and had to endure the same treatment. He reckoned our father knew that if he'd appeared to have shown his sons the slightest suggestion of favouritism, it would have not gone down well with the other boys. This might have made our lives miserable and so he went to the other extreme instead. I ended up asking my father about it. He said he hated doing it, but he'd rather that we were angry at him than have a tough time from our peers. I came to realise that in a perverse way it was an act of kindness.

'But I see that your situation is more complicated, Xavi. I'm trying to put myself in your father's shoes... if I was suddenly unable to work or contribute to family life, I think I'd feel like a passenger, maybe even a burden. He probably takes out his frustrations on you because he can't be the father he was to you before the accident.'

Andy looked me up and down. 'I mean, if I was confined to a chair and saw you growing into a strong young man, I would probably find that jolly difficult. What I mean to say is, I'd be grumpy as hell if I were him. But listen, I don't know him like you do, but I've seen a glint in his eye. Maybe he's feeling useful again.'

I let Andy's words sink in. I have to say that my first feelings were of shame. Shame at myself for underestimating the degree to which Papa's life had changed following the accident. I hadn't thought through the miseries of what he must be experiencing. And felt ashamed because I had indeed noticed a hint of the old Papa recently, and I hadn't tried to involve him. Still, I was grateful to Andy for giving me a clearer understanding of just how wretched life had become for my unfortunate father.

The arrival of the war in our little corner of France had certainly changed things for all of us. I didn't know then how profound and terrible these changes would soon become.

Chapter Three

L iving in the caves sounded rather prehistoric to us. We teased Andy and Denny about being cavemen. They agreed that it sounded comical and, one day, they would enjoy telling their grandchildren about their experiences as troglodytes. Mind you, they reckoned they were a lot better off than their comrades who were probably holed up in some makeshift shelter in the woods. They were eating like kings, and they looked forward to every culinary delight that was brought up to them daily. In addition, they thought that being able to have a leisurely bath twice a week was almost like being at home. Of course, these were not without risk from surprise visitors.

The water for the baths had to be heated in the kitchen and taken up to the bathroom in buckets. The two Englishmen took it in turns to bathe first and enjoy the clean water. Next man in had to put up with little bits of mud and other particles of I'm not sure what floating in it. However, for both men, it was an opportunity to luxuriate in hot, clean (or less clean) water. While this went on, either Mama or I were in the corridor outside the bathroom with the door open at the top of the stairs down to the garden. The other one of us was downstairs keeping watch from the front door to warn of unwanted callers.

On one occasion, Denny was reading a book in the sitting room, while Mama was busy with her housework downstairs. I was sweeping the corridor on the first- floor landing and Andy was splashing about in the bath. Then we heard it. The throaty roar of Günther's motorbike made us jump with fright – except on this occasion it wasn't Günther, it was Otto. He applied the brake, the tyres scrunched kicking up a lot of dust. The man was in a hurry. Oh, my God. Help!

We had agreed in case of immediate evacuation the assembly point would be the spinney where they had arrived in the early hours a short while ago. Denny did not need telling. He picked up his book and disappeared as fast he could towards the spinney. Shortly afterwards, Otto burst through the front door, brushed Mama aside who attempted to engage him in conversation and galloped up the stairs. The man WAS in a hurry. What a minute earlier had been a normal, mundane but, under the circumstances, keenly awaited event, had in the blink of an eye been transformed into a matter of life or death.

At the sound of the motorbike, I had heard Andy shout out one word which was probably the English equivalent of 'merde'. The splashing noises stopped abruptly as I rushed to the bathroom door. Andy had stood up in the bath, his face a picture of alarm. There was no time to exchange any words. I returned to the corridor and said good afternoon to the major. I got a grunt in return, as he strode past me into his room. Mama had brought up earlier a pile of freshly laundered towels which she had put on a chair in the corner of the landing.

Otto emerged from the bedroom clutching a bag which presumably contained what he had left behind and walked past the bathroom to the top of the stairs. Relief flooded through me, and I took a breath for the first time in what felt like a minute. But wait. The major seemed to have a sudden thought and stopped in his tracks. He put the bag down, turned round and opened the door into the bathroom – the same bathroom where Andy was at that moment standing in the tub!

I felt all the colour drain from my face and scrunched my eyes shut, waiting for the inevitable uproar that would signal our probable execution. But there were no shouts. I cautiously moved towards the door that the major had left slightly ajar, and through the gap I watched Otto methodically washing his hands and face at the basin. As he turned off the taps and looked in the mirror above the basin, his attention was grabbed by the draining bath and the water gathered in what looked like footprints on the floor. He paused briefly as if to look for an explanation.

Where on earth was Andy? The only place he could be was in the cupboard in the corner – could he really have got in there so quickly? Sure enough as I peered closer, I could see some drops of water by the cupboard door. Finding the bath unoccupied, the major seemed to remember the urgency with which he returned to the house. He finished washing his face and looked for a towel to dry himself but there wasn't one there, and to my horror I saw him take a couple of steps and reach towards the door of the cupboard.

'Major!' I cried, my voice as loud and high-pitched as I'd ever heard it. 'Major. There are no towels there.' He was clearly not expecting his ablutions to be interrupted in such a way, and came towards the door, his face a picture of anger.

I have never moved as fast in my eighty long years as I did that morning when I dashed to the chair with the towels on it and scooped one of them up, as well as a mop which was propped up in the corner. I handed the towel to the major with an apologetic smile and then started to vigorously mop up the water on the floor. I was trying to give the impression that I had been in the middle of cleaning it and the bath when he showed up. At that moment, Mama appeared, as natural as you like, in the doorway to check on my cleaning. My goodness, how our hearts were thumping as we stood there.

There was another growl from Otto as he dried his face and then left the bathroom striding back down the stairs. We held our breath until the engine of the motor bike burst into life. Mama and I sat on the edge of the bath with both arms and legs shaking, sucking in great gulps of air in blessed relief. At that moment, a gentle knocking noise emanated from the cupboard. A still wet and sheepish Andy emerged from his captivity. He looked badly shaken, stiff from his short incarceration and was still totally naked. Mama looked away in embarrassment as

I thrust a towel at him so that he could cover his modesty. Nobody spoke for a while. Our minds were still full of the enormity of what had just happened and our brush with almost certain death.

The silence was broken by Mama who started praying out loud, thanking God for our deliverance. Just then we heard movement downstairs and footsteps on the stairs. Oh, My God! Had Otto seen through my deception and summoned reinforcements?

An English voice said loudly from downstairs. 'Just wondering whether you're all still alive?' It was Denny. He too had heard the motorbike and assumed that the coast was clear. We had last seen him what seemed like an eternity ago but was in fact only five minutes. We related what had happened. Andy, a towel now firmly around his waist, shook me by the hand, then embraced me and said 'Thank you, Xavi, for saving my life. It was your quick thinking that did it.' Mama looked at me and beamed proudly. Andy said. 'Talk about being caught with your trousers down.' With that, the tension was released as we realised now that tragedy had so narrowly been averted, just how comical the situation was. We laughed until the tears started rolling down our cheeks.

Much to our relief, nothing was said at supper that night. In fact, if it was possible, Otto was positively effusive with his conversation. He told us, via Günther's interpreting, about some of his exploits hunting wild boar in Bavaria.

On our next visit to the caves, Mama announced that Denny's arm was looking better, and he could start being a bit more active. So, he came and joined us on the roof of the cave. I mentioned to the others that Papa and Philippe had been talking about the maquis and how they were disorganised, unreliable and untrustworthy.

Andy said he had had first-hand experience of this when he, his commanding officer and twenty-one others had landed by parachute on 1st September. When he landed there was absolute chaos. One of the supply containers' parachutes failed to open and exploded on impact which made the trigger-happy maquisards who were part of the reception committee think they were being attacked by the Germans. They all opened fire at goodness knows what, and this meant that the drop zone had been compromised and needed to be evacuated as quickly as possible. In the ensuing furore, some of the British parachutists got separated from the main body. Yes, said Andy, they were very much all those things.

I added that with the word 'untrustworthy', Philippe had not just necessarily meant that they could not be trusted to do the right thing but also in the sense that their loyalty was dubious. The maquis was riddled with informants and spies. As fiercely patriotic Frenchmen, both Papa and Philippe were ashamed of their fellow countrymen. 'These spies will be judged when the war is over,' said my mother.

'Are you against spying on principle, Madame?' Denny asked her.

While I certainly knew what a spy was and the idea of running the gauntlet of the enemy in trying to obtain valuable information was exciting to a ten-year-old boy,

I had never really considered what drove people to risk torture and death to carry it out.

Patriotism and the doing of one's duty were laudable, according to Mama. Denny thought that the issue of divided loyalties, especially here in the Vosges where the border was occasionally redrawn after a major conflict, made spying understandable. 'For some, political beliefs are more important than lines drawn on a map or even loyalty to one's country,' argued Andy. However, Mama maintained that to conduct espionage for the sake of financial gain was the most heinous reason of them all and entirely deserving of the death penalty.

Andy turned to me, a hint of a smile on his lips. 'I have a story to tell you about spying.' I raised an interested eyebrow.

'You know at school we all slept in dormitories. They varied in size, but I suppose the average was six boys. The night was the only time during the whole twenty-four hours that we were unsupervised so that was the time we got up to our mischief. Father put the lights out at 8.30pm most evenings. A matron used to come round at 11.00pm shining a torch on every bed to check that every bed was occupied by the correct occupant. If something was planned for later, we all feigned sleep.

'During the time that I was at the family school there were some superb story tellers, not just the teachers but also the boys. It was a great treat some nights to lie in bed and listen to tales of derring-do, war and ghosts. Depending on the skill of the narrator, there were times when sleep claimed you before the denouement or if the story really gripped you, you were wider awake than when you started. There was one story that stood out from all the others.'

Andy stopped and cleared his throat. I thought to myself after the build-up that this might be another of his teases when he says that's all for now but apparently not on this occasion.

'We had an elderly member of staff at the school called Miss Snickel who was always referred to by the boys as Ma Snick. She terrified the living daylights out of us and ruled us with a rod of iron. She occupied a small bedroom at the very top of the house which, because it was so high, had sensational views of the coast, sea and a famous lighthouse guarding some treacherous rocks.

'When it was dark, the light beam from the lighthouse would flash towards us intermittently as it swept around the horizon alerting ships to the danger. We were convinced by the story's first-rate narrator that the winking light of this lighthouse was in fact a signal sent by a German spy to Ma Snick. The Great War had been over for a few years but we, as ten-year-olds, were still obsessed by it or maybe somehow, we had cottoned on to the idea that Germany was in fact rearming ready for '39. We thought that Ma Snick was an enemy agent also and was communicating to her contact across the water by a very powerful torch. Dot, dash, Dash, dot, etc.

'We were also convinced that she was really a man. Her hair was a wig. She had a deepish voice and was hirsute. She had a decent moustache, worthy of the Kaiser himself. Mind you there were several other lady members of staff who had one of those too. When we took our books up to her desk in class, we would always stand behind her and peer down the inside of her shirt or dress to see there were any signs of body hair.

'Xavi, you might be asking yourself what on earth could an elderly lady at an isolated boys' school provide in the way of useful information to the German High Command? Well, one thing is for sure we did have some boys whose fathers were high ranking officers in the army, navy, air force, officials in the War Office and even one ambassador. Indeed, the son of the Air Chief Marshall in charge of Bomber Command was a pupil at the school. On Sundays at school, all the boys had to write a letter home. It so happened that all the letters were censored or vetted by Ma Snick herself.

'The reason for this was that the school did not want the parents to know whether their child was being bullied, was very unhappy or the food was vile. Ma Snick would supervise the letter writing and, according to her, needed the most recent letter from home (usually from the child's mother) in order that she could advise each child what to write. The letters of particular interest to her were from the high-ranking military families. Comments like 'Daddy has just been posted to Gibraltar to take command of a brand spanking new battleship, HMS Nelson,' or 'Daddy's just been made Colonel of 1st Battalion, Welsh Guards and has been posted to Cyprus' or 'Daddy's just been down to Dorset to see a new tank that is being developed. It's very advanced and hush hush' were like nuggets of gold to her. Whenever these parents would come down to school to visit their sons, we would watch Ma Snick go sidling up to them trying to eavesdrop on their conversation. You can just imagine Ma Snick making notes about what she had heard, ready for a busy session with her high-powered torch that evening.

'There were also rumours of a secret staircase ready for a quick getaway if it were needed. If you pulled up the floorboards in her bedroom, it would reveal an entrance with metal rungs on it descending into the blackness beneath. The exit to the staircase was apparently above the doorway into the school dining room. This to us appeared entirely feasible because above the door there were two smaller ones suggesting there was some cupboard or even a long narrow passage behind them. Also in the dining room were three large family portraits from the 18th century with substantial gilded frames. One of these portraits hung over one of the tables at which the ten-year-olds sat and ate their food.

'The painting in question was of an elderly lady of Ma Snick's age. She was dressed in black with a white bonnet and lace finery around the neck and on the lapels. If you looked hard enough at one of the eyes, it would blink. The story was that Ma Snick was literally keeping an eye on us at mealtimes also. More important still, it was a good vantage point from which to overhear important conversations between parents at some of the evening dinners that Father used to lay on. Politics, defence issues as well as the latest antics of Winston Churchill would have been hot topics at the dining table. Ma Snick was undoubtedly hoping to add to her tally of golden nuggets.

'When I was older and no longer taught by this terrifying lady, I once asked Father whether he knew that one of his staff was a man dressed as a woman and a German spy. I had to relate what I am telling you. While I was doing this, his face remained deadpan although I did observe a momentary twitch of the lips. However, he neither confirmed nor denied the story. What I do know is that Ma Snick is still at the school but, if she is a spy, she would have to find a new contact to pass information on. In early 1940, the school was evacuated several hundred miles to the north, well away from the south coast and the threat of German invasion.'

That's one for the diary I thought as I made my way home. I was itching to tell Mama and Papa about Andy's story. However, we had a visitor. There were voices coming from Papa's study. I knocked on the door. It was Philippe Mercier who was with him and surprise, surprise they were discussing village war gossip and what he had gleaned from the latest BBC broadcasts. When he left, Papa told us that the Americans should be here any day now but that the Germans were still hunting down the British paratroopers. No change there then, I thought to myself. I said to Papa that the Americans had been expected any day now for a while. Did he think something had gone wrong? His answer was that these things rarely go to plan, so we all just must be patient. He paused for a moment and then announced theatrically that he had one more piece of information. A message had at long last come through for our English guests. It ran 'STAY WHERE YOU ARE AND AWAIT DEVELOPMENTS'. I said that I would deliver it to them tomorrow.

Mama was in her usual place preparing food for the various households for which she was now responsible. We had to slip from our double life into our treble life for the evening, making sure that anything destined to go 'up the hill' so to speak was kept out of view. Conversation with the major was usually kept to the bare minimum: the most we normally got out of him was 'Good evening' and when it was all over 'Good night'. Mama rarely got thanked for the meal. However, on this occasion, using gangly Günther as interpreter, obdurate Otto, as we had christened him had rather more to say for himself. From under the table, he produced with a slight flourish and a large grin, a bag of English tobacco. Mama and I were rather taken aback. Was he hinting at something? Was this the precursor to arresting us for helping the enemy. Much to our relief, the answer was provided quickly. They had found the tobacco, which was clearly not to their taste, in parachuted containers in the forests that had gone astray in a misdirected resupply drop. They wished to trade the tobacco for fresh eggs laid by our hens. So, the deal was done.

After this bit of excitement, the major lapsed back into his old ways. He attacked his food which was followed by the customary belch, perhaps his idea of a compliment. Günther on the other hand had barely started to eat and was eager to engage us in conversation but was still reserved in his superior's presence. When Otto disappeared off to bed, Günther told us he had received a letter from home. There was still no news of his brother in the U boat which was not good. His parents were now fearing the worst. Heidelberg had been indiscriminately bombed by the Americans.

With no attempt at bombing only military targets, they had struck at historic buildings and populated areas of the city; the famous medieval castle and the beautiful old bridge had been badly damaged. Two houses in the same street where his parents lived had received direct hits. Although the sirens had gone off, the occupants had been unable to get to the relative safety of the shelters and several of their neighbours had been killed. The letter had ended with them imploring their son, probably their only surviving one, to come back to them safely.

Mama offered the poor man another glass of wine. For the first time he had let his guard slip. He said, lowering his voice to a whisper, the war was as good as lost and that he had been sceptical about Adolf Hitler and the Nazi party all along. There were many of his fellow countrymen who shared the same views as he did, but they also knew what would happen to them if their disloyalty became known. He feared for his parents, his way of life and his country. The only way to avert catastrophe was for Germany to surrender unconditionally.

He stopped abruptly and looked up at us, clearly wondering if he had said too much. He took a deep breath and shook his head a few times to compose himself. Eventually he mumbled that the anxiety he felt about his brother in the submarine service and his parents at the mercy of American bombers had made him say things he did not really believe.

There was a pause. Mama chose her words carefully. 'This war is terrible and you didn't choose it any more than we did.

'The best antidote for worry I know of,' she continued, 'is music. Why don't you go and play the piano for us. I will go and fetch my husband and we can listen. How about some Debussy, Chopin or Saint-Saëns?'

As we gathered in front of the piano, the silence punctuated by Günther's melodious tones, another thought occurred to me. This was now a new secret we had to keep. Not only did we have two British soldiers hiding in the woods who we were harbouring but now we had a tough, hard-bitten Nazi billeted in our house with a frightened and homesick colleague who had just spoken out vehemently against Hitler. It had just occurred to me that Günther's outburst could be used as a bargaining tool if needed. Life in the Le Rolland house might have been playing out like a light farce but at least it wasn't dull.

The next morning, Mama and I passed on the message that Monsieur Mercier had brought. The two Englishmen were pleased that communication had at last been established but disappointed it meant yet more inaction. Mama said that far more important than anything to do with the war was that today was her birthday and we were going to celebrate it. We were going to have a birthday lunch up here at the caves. She would also bring a couple of bottles of suitably nice wine. While she was looking at Denny's arm, Andy asked me whether there were any wildflowers in the vicinity. If not, might there be some flowers in our garden that could somehow find their way up to the caves.

'Let's cobble together something floral,' he said.

After she left, Andy and I went in search. The higher we climbed; the trees were more thinly spread. This meant it was lighter and the chance of finding flowers was greater. Andy became briefly like a child on a treasure hunt, squawking with excitement when he thought he saw something suitable. We found a plentiful supply of small purple and white … something. We had no idea what they were, they were just flowers. We picked some and made them into a small bouquet.

On the roof of the cave, the view was as spectacular as ever but there was a chill in the air, reminding us that autumn was not far away. When he said that Mama bringing the wine had given him an idea for a post lunch entertainment, I noticed not for the first time that he was fiddling with what looked like a small coin. I asked him about it. 'It's an English sixpenny piece,' he said. 'It's not worth very much but it reminds me of home and is, I suppose, a kind of St Christopher or worry bead. I feel I must play with it all the time, especially when I'm desperate for a smoke and I can't have one because I'm running out of tobacco. I don't know what I would do if I lost it because I am a great fiddler. I find it helps me when I get anxious.' He handed me the little silver coin. It looked smooth and shiny. I could just about make the head of the English king, whose name I tried to remember.

I returned to our house in good time to help Mama get the lunch ready. She had prepared a veritable feast – homemade pâté de campagne, some saucisson made by Monsieur Villemin, the butcher in the village, and several different types of cheese, olives, tomatoes and crusty bread. The pièce de resistance was her legendary tarte aux poires. I scooped everything up including the wine and the bag containing the tobacco. Together we trudged up the well-trodden path up the hillside to the caves. Denny had tidied up the 'dining area' in front of the cave (or more likely just shoved all their stuff out of sight). Both men had evidently made a bit of an effort to smarten themselves up. I realised how much Andy's hair had grown by the way he swept it to one side.

Mama laid the lunch out. We had all made ourselves as comfortable as we could be, bearing in mind we had rocks for seats. Andy had uncorked the wine and we were just about to drink a toast when Mama asked for silence. I recognised that impish look on her face. Mama liked to tease. She nonchalantly asked them how their supply of tobacco was lasting. 'We're smoking dust, now you mention it,' said Andy.

The fighting men of any nation, she said, who could put up with any hardship, to be deprived of their 'smokes' was the ultimate morale buster. I shall never forget how their faces lit up with pleasure and relief when, with a conjuror's flourish, she produced a bag of tobacco from her bag and explained how she had come about it. Denny would now be able to fill his pipe and Andy roll his cigarettes and suddenly anything would be possible in this world. All courtesy of a senior member of the Wehrmacht.

That really set the tone for a very happy lunch. When Denny handed over the bunch of wildflowers, we all sang her 'Happy Birthday' in both languages. I lost count of the number of toasts that were drunk. We certainly raised our glasses to absent friends, family and loved ones, the generosity, kindness and courage of the Le Rolland family, the regiment, Winston Churchill, Charles de Gaulle, true Resistance fighters and the soonest possible demise of Adolf Hitler. The lunch was demolished and, unsurprisingly, the tarte aux poires received rave reviews. The wine too was going down well. We had just started the second bottle whereupon Andy took a swig, smiled and asked Mama whether any of us had sampled any wines from North Africa – Algeria or Morocco in particular? Mama couldn't recall but Denny, who seemed to know about these things, said he had and some of them were good stuff.

Andy said he had asked that question for a good reason. 'Will you indulge a slightly tipsy Englishman by listening to another story?' We were all too eager to listen, even if the food and drink had made us drowsy.

'Remember Ma Snick's lighthouse?'. We all nodded, including Mama who had enjoyed the story when I relayed it to her. 'It was built to warn sailors of the dangerous ridge of rocks that ran out to sea opposite our beach. These rocks were a major hazard to shipping which over the years had given many vessels a watery grave.

'Well, one day at the end of the Christmas holidays, a cargo ship was wrecked there – in rather mysterious circumstances. From the edge of the cliff with the aid of a telescope we had a grandstand view of what was happening. We watched with great excitement the arrival of the lifeboat which, by virtue of some tricky manoeuvres, heroically managed to rescue the crew.

The salvage experts tried several times to tow the ship off the rocks but to no avail. She was well and truly stuck.

'We discovered later that she had been carrying thousands of oranges from North Africa as well as five hundred or so barrels of wine. The removal of the cargo was a delicate operation, took several months and was only partially successful. The poor old ship remained stuck astride these rocks battered by storms. They eventually took their toll and caused a hole to appear in her side, inviting the sea in. The swirling action of the waves easily picked up the baskets of oranges and finally the barrels of red wine were liberated also, as Father put it.'

Andy paused for a moment to check that none of us had succumbed to the effects of the wine and nodded off.

'One of the benefits of living as close to the sea as we did and having virtually our own private beach, was walking along it directly after a storm. Over the years, we had found many items washed up and it was always a case of finders, keepers.

'However, nothing had prepared us for the sight that greeted us every day for several weeks. It was unbelievable. The sea had breached the cargo ship's hull and instead of pebbles on our beach as far as the eye could see, it was now festooned by thousands of oranges. The boys and teachers ate nothing but oranges for days. We hardly ever had snow on our cliff top location, meaning we missed out on snowball fights. So, we had orange fights instead.

'While the teachers were pleased by the unexpected bounty of the oranges and their health benefits, it was – surprise, surprise – the casks of wine that were getting them exercised. However, there was one problem; how to get the heavy casks up the steep cliffs. Father, who was not by any stretch of the imagination a practical man, had to defer that task to one of the teachers. Poor Mr Jennings had his leg pulled by his colleagues who joked that he was descended from a family of smugglers so he would know what to do.

'I couldn't tell you how we did it. The barrels had to be pushed or rolled across thirty or so yards of undulating shingle, before being hauled and pulled for another forty or so yards up a seventy-degree slope covered in low scrub. A huge ask physically, but just about possible with a labour force of sixty-five boys, eight male teachers, handymen and gardeners. Even the old boy who came to tend to the roses lent a hand.

'Just to add to the drama, it was imperative that the whole operation be done quickly and, if possible, secretly. As soon as the barrels of wine were washed ashore, officials from an unpopular government organisation called Customs and Excise would come along and stave them in, allowing their delicious contents to drain away into the sand.'

Mama was dumbfounded at the apparent stupidity of this act and demanded to know the reason why. 'Taxes,' said Andy.

'Jesus wept,' said my mother. 'There would be a riot if this happened in France.'

Andy continued with the story. 'So, Father was pacing up and down, yelling encouragement at the staff and boys, checking everyone was safe. His enthusiasm was infectious and before long we had everybody singing sea shanties, pirate songs and cries of YO, HEAVE, HO. But suddenly this chorus of voices went silent when disaster nearly struck.

'Just as the next foursome of burly boys was about to take over, the knot tying the ropes had worked itself loose and the barrel started to roll downwards. Father yelled 'watch out!'. Three of the boys reacted quickly and leapt out of the way as it careered down the cliff. The fourth froze like a rabbit in the headlights. Father, showing remarkable agility for a man of his age, hurled himself at the boy and pulled him out of the path of the speeding barrel, which eventually came to rest in a large bush of brambles. A dashed close-run thing!'

Father described the whole scene later as a scene from a biblical story or Ancient Greece, like the wooden horse of Troy being pulled by vast numbers of sweaty warriors. It was just another example, he said, of locals trying to outwit the 'revenue men' that had been played out over the years along stretches of British coastlines following shipwrecks.

'Anyway, finally, to cries of delight and much backslapping, we teased the barrel onto the top of the cliff, and once it was secured, everybody collapsed. But the burning question was of course – was the wine drinkable? Or was this exercise the biggest folly since the charge of the Light Brigade?

'The answer to that question came when we saw some rather pale teachers clutching their heads the following morning. Despite the unusual nature of the task, Father was proud of his boys and teachers, and the way they had worked together to achieve something that initially was thought to be impossible. Even the parents partook of the illegal booty at the school's annual Speech Day where glasses were raised to 'His Majesty's Customs and Excise. May they never know anything about it.'

The audience of three gave Andy a well-deserved round of applause. Mama said what a good raconteur Andy was, which elicited more clapping. Denny, ever the wine buff, wanted to know more about the wine, which apparently was smooth, medium bodied and extremely drinkable.

I had been swept away by the story for all sorts of reasons, one of which was that the setting of the beach, shingle, waves, ships even was so far removed from my world of forests and mountains.

I was irresistibly drawn to stories of the sea, its vastness and secrecy stirring something in me, despite the fact I had only ever seen it in photographs. Living as we all were in a time of war, I'm sure that most boys of my age had wondered when whether we would become a soldier, sailor or airman. Because of my fascination with the sea, I had always thought I would join the navy. Maxence too was keen to go to sea while Aurélien was destined for the army and terra firma. I was desperate to learn more about Andy and Denny's part in the war before they dropped into our valley. I had pestered Andy to tell me about it. So, when we were packing up after Andy's story, I reminded him how keen I was to learn what action they had seen.

Andy said. 'It's Denny's turn to play narrator. His story is far more interesting than mine.'

That evening at supper, Mama was feeling rather brave and decided to ask, via Günther, whether Otto had any idea of for how much longer we would be having the pleasure of their company. Günther appeared astounded and asked whether Mama really meant that. We knew that the German people were not big on humour but surprised that Günther hadn't really understood the way it was meant. Mama then told him to ask Otto more formally.

Otto gave a curt response which didn't need translating. No was the answer and it's none of your business how long we stay. As usual, we all heaved a collective sigh of relief when Otto headed upstairs (and that included Günther). I poured him another glass of wine. We asked him about his ability with the piano. Apparently, he was the first serious musician in the family and had discovered his ability by accident. A good friend near him in Heidelberg had a piano which his mother used to play. She began to teach him and was amazed by his natural ability. Before the war started, he had just started playing professionally until he was called up. He hated the army and admitted that he could not wait for peace to break out and for his return to the concert hall. We made a pact there and then. If we all came through the war unscathed, we said somewhat half-heartedly that we would love to see him play in a concert. He thought it an excellent idea and we shook hands on the deal. Whatever happened, we would remember Günther with fondness.

Chapter Four

Denny was on the mend. Although his arm was still painful and needed a daily check-up from Mama, he was up and about more. He felt able to make a greater contribution to the daily routine and help with some of the chores. As a result, I spent more time with him, and we got along fine despite the language barrier. Where Andy was tall and lean, Denny was squat and thickset, with a strong jaw and eyes that would not take any nonsense. As a major, he outranked Andy – a captain – and occasionally it showed. After all, he was second in command of the operation. They were tough paratroopers and, being English, were reluctant to show their feelings. Yet, it was clear that Andy was devoted to his senior officer, and not just out of duty either. Although he mentioned it only once in my earshot, Denny realised that he owed his life to Andy.

Denny had born his wound bravely. He was used to injuries and broken bones because he was an accomplished horseman. In fact, he was a 'jump jockey', a steeplechaser well-known in amateur circles. His was a dangerous sport, as falling off was common-place and so were broken limbs. He had lost count of the number of times he had broken his wrists and collar bone. His recovery from his wounded arm had undoubtedly been delayed by all the tiny faultlines in the bone, according to Mama.

Now that Denny was 'back on games' as Andy called it, their thoughts inevitably started to turn to re-joining the fight. They were both conscious that the war had been going on without them and they were desperate to kill a few Germans. The trouble was that they had no means of contacting the remainder of the group. Besides which, the area was swarming with the enemy who were determined to keep the Allies from breaking through on to the German soil of the Fatherland. With the Americans expected any day, Mama and Papa urged them to stay put until liberation.

Although logic and common sense dictated that staying put was the sensible option, sitting on their backsides was not part of the British character and an anathema to their military ethos. It was clear to them even from their hideout that the mission was not going to plan, and they were badly needed. How would they be able to live with themselves after the war if they were sitting idly by when their comrades were fighting the battle of their lives? It was obvious to us that common sense was not going to win this particular argument, so we resigned ourselves that they wouldn't be with us much longer.

One fiercely hot Sunday, I decided to pester Andy and Denny again about their military exploits earlier in the war. When I arrived at the caves, they were already sitting outside the caves in their vests busily cleaning their guns, as if on cue. Denny said that the cleanliness of their weaponry was one of the most important lessons drilled into them from the first day of their training. You never know when you might need them and a reliable, clean gun could be the difference between life and death. Theirs were sten guns and they had a reputation for jamming or misfiring, so even more essential to keep them clean.

Denny could see that I was interested and asked Andy to translate. 'The most important tool of our trade is our gun. Killing Germans is what we are here to do and this is what we do it with,' said Denny affectionately patting the sten gun as if it were a treasured pet. I must admit, it wasn't the most beautiful piece of machinery. It looked as though it had hastily been put together by a plumber using spare parts from his toolbag. As if reading my mind, Denny said 'she's not a looker but if she's well looked after, she can be a trusted and damned lethal companion. She can fire five hundred rounds a minute and being a submachine gun, can be devastating in close quarter fighting which is very much our trade.

Do you want to hold it, Xavi? It's not loaded, of course.'

So, for the first and only time in my life, I held a submachine gun. The steel was hot to touch having been in the sun and far heavier than I imagined. The other two probably thought I was a bit puerile but I couldn't help pulling the trigger and noisily pretending to spray bullets in all directions. 'Take that, you dirty doryphores', I said as I blew imaginary smoke from the tip. 'I've just shot seven Germans' I shouted gleefully.

'Well done, lad!' said Denny thumping me on the back. 'I'd better take that back before you get too attracted to it. And for goodness' sake don't tell your mother or she'll send us packing.'

Somewhat reluctantly I gave the gun back and asked Denny about their parachuting. How did they learn to do it without ending up as strawberry jam?

Denny smiled. 'Dropping soldiers by parachute with their weapons is still a new science, so the training is, how can I put it, feeling its way a little.'

He beckoned to Esmé to come over and lie down near him. The golden retriever did not need to be asked twice. For the last week or so, Esmé had been Denny's constant companion and it was clear that the two of them were besotted with each other. The major gave her a pat and then continued while Andy translated for my benefit.

'Our training course lasted two weeks, and before we started, I'd never been higher than the Eiffel tower, but they taught us well. As we learned, the trickiest and most important part of operating a parachute successfully and safely is the landing. We practiced over and over again on different terrain and in different weather conditions and blimey, you don't want to be jumping out of a plane on a gusty day.

'Seconded', said Andy.

Denny went on, 'even for experienced paratroopers it's very easy to break a leg if you don't land right – you need to fall and roll in as compact a body position as possible.' He looked round. 'It's easier to see it in action perhaps we can persuade my beautiful assistant, Andy, to demonstrate?'

Andy laughed and saluted.

On the outside of the cave, he found a rock at the right height from the ground and a soft level landing place – not an easy task on a craggy hillside. Together we dragged one of their mattresses out of the caves to cushion our falls. They both made it clear they were going to be extremely cautious because any sort of injury would be disastrous for them and for their desire to re-join the fight. Andy took up a position on the rock which at the very most was only twenty inches off the ground. His knees were slightly bent, his elbows tucked in, his chin depressed into his neck and his hands raised as if to hold on to part of the chute. From this position he jumped, then when his feet hit the mattress, he rolled to the right, keeping his limbs close to his body.

Typical of the man, he sat up and said with a wink, 'as easy as getting out of bed in the morning.' Of course, it wasn't. The idea of the roll, I learned, was to spread as much of the impact as possible to all parts of the body and avoid breaking your ankle.

Andy then teased Denny by saying that he was better at falling than most because he was so used to being chucked off his horse.

Denny rolled his eyes. 'So, when the trainers were convinced you were ready, the next stage in the parachuting training programme was jumping from a hot air balloon nine hundred feet above ground. At the place where you collected your chute it was hard not to be a little disconcerted by a sign that read 'REMEMBER THAT A MAN'S LIFE DEPENDS ON EVERY PARACHUTE YOU PACK.' I hoped that the person that had packed mine hadn't just had a heavy night drinking. Muttering a few prayers, we were winched up to the hot air balloon with three other trainees and there, as nervous as hell, awaited our turn. Boy, do I remember my first time."

I could see Denny reliving it, his eyes wide with a nervous excitement.

'The instructor said 'Go' and suddenly the earth was racing towards me at two hundred kilometres an hour, the wind whistling through my nose. Just when I was convinced I was going to end up pâté de Reynolds on the ground, it felt like two massive hands gripped my shoulders, slowing me down. And then like a miracle this huge beautiful white parachute bloomed above, guiding me back to the ground. Luckily after all that landing practice, I managed that part quite well, just missing a hedgerow thick with brambles.'

I winced at the idea. Denny went on. 'The course was finished with five jumps from an actual aircraft. In our case this was done from an elderly bomber, reassuringly nicknamed the flying coffin.'

Mama snorted at this.

'And, fittingly, it didn't feel particularly safe. The noise in the aircraft during take-off was enough to shatter your ear drums, and then the whole thing shuddered and juddered in the air – it felt like a paper kite in a hurricane. But if you were lucky enough to survive all five jumps, including one at night, you received your wings badge and the famous maroon beret. I think I must have walked with a real swagger the first time I wore that out of camp.'

Denny paused and flexed the fingers of his left hand to make sure they weren't stiffening up. He looked up at me and asked me whether one day I would like to become a parachutist in the French Army. I said that now I would rather keep my feet firmly on the ground. Denny then asked me if I wanted to hear a bit about his first parachute operation on enemy soil. Did he need to ask?

'Just over a year ago', he said, 'I took part in the invasion of Sicily. Xavi, do you know where that is?'

I shook my head.

'It's a large island off the big toe of the boot of Italy. Our mission was crucial – the Allies wanted to use Sicily as a stepping stone to invade Italy, and our team was tasked with a vital role. So, we found ourselves in North Africa for training, preparing for what lay ahead.

'In Sicily, our target was an important bridge across a river, and we were to be dropped a few miles inland from the coast. The plan was to capture and secure the objective. But there was a worrisome twist – the enemy might try to blow up the bridge once our troops and tanks landed on the beach. That could cause a massive bottleneck and delay the whole island's capture.

'We only had a few hours' notice that we were going, and everything had to be crammed into our pockets. Maps, money, compasses, medical kit, and an escape pack – we had to be prepared for anything. The briefing we got was complex and included detailed codes and messages.

We had just half an hour to digest all the information before the action.

'As we boarded the plane, I was in command of a stick of ten brave men. We were all ready to face the challenges that lay ahead. Our sten guns were secured in containers, but we carried Colt 45 revolvers as our trusty companions. One of our men even had a carrier pigeon hidden inside his smock, just in case the radios failed.

'As we soared above the coast of Sicily that night, any romantic notions about a peaceful descent through the sky vanished. Chaos had erupted below us. Anti-aircraft guns had already taken down some of our planes, and we later learned that other members of our battalion were dropped in the wrong places.

'The moon illuminated the night sky, meaning the visibility was good. Too good, as it turned out. Suddenly, we saw streaks of tracer bullets, and I realised we were a target to be aimed at. It was a terrifying moment, but I had to remind myself that I was in command of this plane load of men and must not show any weakness.

'Far off to the right, the sky was lit by a sudden heavy barrage. We saw the coast. This was Sicily – we were close to our drop zone. But suddenly, the pilot had to take evasive action and we were thrown from our seats. Then came the order through my intercom that we should get ready to jump. We put on our helmets and adjusted our straps.

'A few seconds later from the front came the cry. 'Green light. Jump!' We scrambled forward, one after the other and leaped out into the blackness. My heart pounded as I flung myself forward and felt the force of the slipstream. But after what felt like an age, the parachute opened, and that feeling of relief washed over me. I checked the stick's direction, watched the drift, and counted the chutes.

'But I noticed that things were not going as planned. I didn't recognise the terrain below, and it turned out we had been dropped in the wrong place. The stick's formation broke up, and I saw other parachutes gliding away. But I had no time to worry as the ground was speeding towards me.

'I grabbed the rigging lines, prepared for impact, and pulled myself up at the right moment. I rolled to the right as I landed and found myself in a patch of cut grass in a field. A wave of euphoria swept over me – I had landed safely. And it was my best landing ever!'

Andy, still translating, looked as gripped as I was.

'We had arranged to meet all the men who were involved in our part of the operation at the entrance to the bridge, but because of the chaos above the drop zone, many never arrived. The first target we were to aim for was two concrete defensive positions – we called them pillboxes – which were guarding the southern side of the bridge. On the way, we met a patrol of four Italians who were immediately shot.'

At this, Denny, who had been looking out towards the setting sun as he spoke, turned and scanned my face, checking this last piece of information hadn't upset me. 'Go on,' I whispered.

He nodded and cleared his throat. 'A grenade was thrown into one of the pillboxes, and fourteen Italians poured out, hands in the air, desperately surrendering. I was then ordered by the officer who had assumed command to take some men and look for any cables linked to demolition charges and cut them immediately.

'The Italian Army was not renowned for its bravery, having surrendered in their thousands in North Africa at the first sign of any difficulty. We used to joke that Italian tanks were equipped with three reverse gears – because they were so used to retreating – and one forward gear in case the enemy launched a surprise attack from the rear. But we knew German units were a different story – organised, brave, and battle-hardened.

'While we were searching for demolition charges, we stumbled upon some empty pillboxes. It seemed like the Italians had already high-tailed it out of there. After finishing cutting the cable, we started heading back south when out of nowhere, three enemy lorries came speeding towards us. Without hesitation, one of our chaps leaped up from his hiding spot and chucked a grenade at the front truck. Boom! It hit dead-on, and all three vehicles went up in flames. They must've been loaded with petrol and ammunition because the fire raged on throughout the night.'

It was getting cold, but I was so entranced by his story that I barely noticed. Denny picked up his pipe and lit it. He seemed suddenly like a different man from the softly spoken one I knew. It reminded me that these two men who had become my friends had other lives, lives in which they commanded men in battle and had probably watched their friends ripped to shreds by gunfire. The thought chilled me.

Now sucking on his pipe, Denny went on. 'The original plan was to secure the bridge until other troops arrived by sea to relieve us. But as the dawn broke, we realised we were spread too thin on the ground, and those troops we were waiting for were nowhere in sight.

'And that's when things took an unexpected turn. Instead of the fleeing Italians, we found ourselves facing a fearsome force – German paratroopers! Can you believe it? Things were going to get very tasty… and tasty they got.

'Throughout the day, we had to face several attacks, including a strafing by Messerschmitt 109s – those were enemy planes, swift and dangerous. We even took some direct hits from a powerful Tiger tank, one of the toughest beasts on the battlefield.'

Andy got up from his chair and went over to the rock from which we had practiced our parachute jumps. He stood on the rock with his legs together and his arms out wide. He then proceeded to do his impersonation of a Messerschmitt on a strafing run, moving both arms up and down and emitting his version of an aero engine and the rat-a-tat-tat of a machine gun. Not to be outdone, Denny then lifted a small tree trunk that was lying on the ground and did his take on a Tiger tank shelling the bridge. Not wishing to be left out, I grabbed a large stick and fired a magazine from my 'sten gun'. What had been a few minutes previously an engrossing and dramatic retelling of part of a crucial battle in the context of the invasion of Sicily had descended into a childish farce but oh, how we laughed.

'What happened in the end? Did you manage to hold the bridge?' I asked when he had recovered.

Denny thought for a moment and said, 'Well, how can I put it... We lost the skirmish, but we won the battle. Don't forget that lots of our men and supplies never actually made it to the bridge. We were lightly armed and unprepared for tanks. When the Italians fled, we knew the Germans would pose a serious threat. We had to retreat from the bridge, but two days later, we regrouped with heavily armed troops, who arrived by sea. Together, we reclaimed the bridge. So, we did it, but like so many things in battle, nothing went as planned.'

We all sat down. There was silence for several minutes. We were all thinking our own thoughts. His story had gripped me but there were so many unanswered questions buzzing around my brain.

'Denny, what did it feel like when you were on that plane getting shot at? And on the ground, was it the first time you fired a shot in battle? Did you kill anybody?'

'Xavi, you can't ask that!', my mother said. Mama had come up to the caves to check on Denny's wound.

'It's fine, Madame', Denny replied. He lit his pipe again, puffing out clouds of smoke. 'At the beginning, there was a lot of excitement. Stepping foot onto Nazi-occupied Europe for the first time, leading the charge as paratroopers, it was a momentous occasion. But let me tell you, that excitement faded quickly as we approached the drop zone and the anti-aircraft fire kicked in.

'And on the ground, I fired my sten a lot and yes some of those shots found their targets, Italian and German. I didn't think much about it at the time nor much afterwards. War, Xavi, it's kill or be killed.'

Denny paused, and Esmé, his loyal companion, trotted over and sat obediently by his side, enjoying the affectionate ear rub he gave her. He had a way with animals, be it dogs or horses. He continued, 'This just reminded me of Tinker, who almost joined us on this mission.' My expression must have revealed my confusion, as I knew Tinker was his beloved black Labrador that accompanied him everywhere back home. 'Believe it or not, Tinker is a trained parachutist and has earned his wings,' Denny said, glancing at Andy for confirmation. Astonishingly, Andy confirmed that the dog had indeed been taught to parachute by its owner. Tinker was all set to join us in the drop into the Vosges, until Colonel Franks himself radioed his deputy and good friend, stating, 'We don't need a bloody dog here."

***

With Denny apparently more like his normal self, it was clear that the two men were getting restless with this period of inertia. It was time, we all agreed, to take some exercise and build up their fitness, a chance to work up some sweat and for Denny specially to rehabilitate himself as a soldier. We decided to kick around an old leather football I had brought along, but finding a flat and open space on the wooded hillside proved challenging. We shared a laugh when one of us misdirected a kick, sending the ball careening over the steep slope and coming to a stop about fifty yards down the hill. That meant a trek down and back up, and in the end, we lost the ball.

I was allowed to join in their physical training sessions which they did most mornings to build up Denny's strength. Exercises to build up stamina in arms, legs, stomach and neck. I could manage at the most twenty repetitions of the star jumps, press ups (only 20 of these for Denny), trunk curls, burpees, lunges and many more, while the men kept going until they reached at least fifty. This was all part of their grand plan to get themselves ready to re-join the fight – a day that I was not looking forward to.

One morning, Andy asked me if I had a small rubber ball anywhere at home. His plan was to introduce me to his beloved cricket. He said it was a strange, eccentric game. 'Peculiarly English' was how he described it. Once he started to explain the rules, I knew what he meant. Apparently, some games could last for five days and even then, you might not get a result. I said it sounded ridiculous.

This, he said, was all part of the English plot to confuse the foreigner. He could tell he was losing me in the detail, so he settled on trying to teach me some of the bizarre terms they use in this sport. I almost choked on the biscuit I was eating when he referred to one of the men in the field as 'fine leg'. It took me quite a few attempts to pronounce the word 'googly' correctly and even after he had explained the concept of an 'innings' three or four times I still had no idea what he was talking about. When the idea of a 'duck' was introduced, I threw a pebble at him and told him to stop pulling my leg.

Denny, who preferred football to cricket, said it was good finally to hear someone talk some sense on the subject.

***

On my next trip up there, there was no talk of games – it was clear something was afoot. Andy and Denny were in a huddle studying maps including the one that Papa had given them. They had obviously cleaned their guns again as they lay glinting in the sun ready for action. The waiting was over. Mama had confirmed to them what they already knew that the nearest important German supply route where they could make a nuisance of themselves was the road between Celles and Raon l'Étape. I looked quizzically at them both. The two men laughed and explained that 'making a nuisance of themselves' was a typical case of English understatement. What they really meant was to kill as many Germans as possible, to shoot up as many vehicles as they could and, ideally, block a major supply route for several days.

Mama said she knew the road well and suggested a place where they could make their presence felt, a spot which provided cover and a relatively straightforward escape route. They decided that as the nights were now drawing in, dusk might be a suitable time to carry out the ambush. Papa, who knew the mountains around here better than most, had only been saying to us both that morning that he thought the weather was going to take a turn for the worse in the next few days. This might serve their purpose. They would carry out a reconnoitre that evening and take stock again tomorrow.

Supper that night assumed an extra significance. Günther seemed less in awe of Otto for some reason. We discussed neutral subjects such as food (a subject dear to Otto's heart), the differences between our respective cuisines. Towards the end of the meal, Günther and Otto had a bit of a discussion between themselves whereupon Günther asked Mama that because they were both aware that she spent a lot of her time preparing food, could they help by contributing to the commissariat. This set a few alarm bells ringing. Did they know something?

After an unusually dry spell, the infamous drizzle that prevails in the Vosges had returned the next morning, as I made my way to their hideout with their tray of food. I was naturally eager to find out how last night's recce had gone and whether they were making use of Father's tarpaulin that he had lent them. While the caves were an ideal shelter at night, they were a gloomy and depressing place to spend the daylight hours. Papa, aware of the fickle nature of the weather in the mountains, had anticipated they might need some rain-proof shelter for that eventuality. Sure enough, they had built an impressive structure.

'Morning, Xavi, what do you think of it?' said Andy, bright and breezy as ever. 'It's Denny's handiwork. It's ingenious, don't you think?'

It certainly was that. What Dennis had created meant that it was possible for them to crawl through the narrow cave opening into the shelter without getting wet. The shelter itself had a roof with two sides, which you could not stand up in, but sitting on the two flimsy wooden chairs they had borrowed from us was possible. The north facing side with that view you could never tire of was open to the elements. The two of them had camouflaged it with small branches of pine and what with the tarpaulin being dark green, the whole extension to their accommodation seemed to blend in well with the surroundings, unlikely to catch the eye of a keen German sentry with binoculars on the other side of the valley.

The two men sat on their chairs eating their breakfast. They were in good spirits and said how civilised the meal was in their new surroundings. Although they only gave a few details, the previous night's outing had gone well. The point on the Celles to Raon l'Étape road that Mama had recommended to them was indeed ideal, they thought. The timings needed some adjustments they because they needed to lie up in good time. Based on what they had seen last night, there had been enough traffic for them to do some damage.

Mama had told me several days ago that Andy's genial, happy go lucky attitude was a bit of a front. He was compensating, she thought, for his anxiety. He had confided in her that the prospect of military action made him edgy. The closer he got to combat the worse it became. For a few hours before actually engaging with the enemy he was, to use his own words, crippled with nerves. However, as soon as the first shot was fired, the adrenaline kicked in and he was raring to go. Andy had asked Mama not to mention this to Denny, who always seemed more relaxed. He dealt with it in his own way, by rigorously studying their plans and cleaning their weapons.

Mama agreed and told me it was entirely normal to feel nervous before military action. You might be killed, for goodness's sake, or your body might sustain terrible wounds. It's really a question of how you deal with it. Many soldiers in the Great War needed at least half a bottle of whisky before they were able to even climb out of their trenches. However, she thought that Andy had it worse than most. She said she thought he would be feeling anxious about this evening's outing and suggested that I might be able to help him by asking him to tell another story. This might distract him from dwelling too much about what may or may not happen that evening.

She didn't need to ask me twice! As soon as I finished my chores, I made my way up to the camp. As much as I loved their tales of battle and life as a soldier, I wanted to hear more about Andy's schooldays. Perhaps it was because of my age at the time or the strains of dealing with Papa but the idea of boarding school fascinated me. I'd never heard of such a thing in France, and I longed to hear about the mischief Andy and his friends got up to and the punishments they faced if they got caught. Andy seemed happier than usual to see me. Denny was getting some sleep, in preparation for their forthcoming ambush and the bivouac shelter kept us dry as Andy started telling me about something called raids.

'A raid was a surprise attack on another dormitory in the middle of the night. The occupants of your dormitory would creep out of bed and armed with your pillows, make your way as quietly as possible to the door of the intended target. You would listen carefully outside the door to make sure that all was quiet. Then, all at once, emitting a controlled shriek, you burst into the room and set upon the comatose occupants with your pillows.

The lighter sleepers amongst them would react quickly, pick up their own pillows and fight back. Sometimes, it developed almost into a pitched battle with slogging duels going on in all corners of the room. Occasionally, a pillow would burst, and feathers would fly everywhere.'

I glimpsed in his smile the young boy in him. 'More often than not,' he went on 'it was the element of surprise that won the day. The attackers might leave a scene of devastation behind them with mattresses upended, sheets ripped off and feathers scattered all over the floor. The thing about raids was you knew at some stage they were going to happen to you, but you weren't sure when, so every night had a slight edge to it. There was an unwritten rule that you were only allowed to raid each dormitory once a term and there were four of them in our part of the school. There were the 'home' and 'away' fixtures which meant a total of six fixtures a term.' He paused and looked up at me. 'Sounds like fun, eh?'

'Yes, it does!' I said, 'Didn't the noise wake any of the grown-ups up though?' I asked.

'Sometimes. The headmaster's bedroom was nearby, as was Matron's. Father was a terrible sleeper. There were some sixty to seventy boys asleep in his school for whom he was totally responsible. It was an old building, and he was obsessively worried about fire. He sometimes lay awake at night thinking he smelt smoke, so he would get up and investigate. He was often padding about the corridors in the middle of the night anyway.

'We all tried to be as quiet as we could but in the heat of battle it was not always possible. If Father did appear, he was at his most terrifying and if you were one of the attackers you knew you would be having a sore bottom for a few days. I know now that he realised deep down that it was a childish prank, a lot of fun and a much-valued part of boarding school life but, of course, as headmaster he could not condone it and would give any guilty party six strokes of the cane. Golly was it painful, but if you did get beaten, you earned respect from your peers. Once I got a good hiding after we carried out a disastrous raid that ended up with a matron being hit in the face by a flying slipper. That day, my pink bottom was a badge of honour.'

I'd noticed that during his story he had been rubbing the coin more vigorously than ever. I said to him that at this rate King George's head would disappear altogether from the side of the coin. Andy replied that it was a few pre-operation nerves. I admitted too that I too was getting nervously excited and wished I was going as an observer. 'Definitely out of the question' he said firmly.

As usual it had been raining and I wondered whether it would make any difference to this evening's entertainment, as he called it. Andy thought, if anything, it would help them because the Germans would not be expecting any attack on such a foul night and would be less vigilant. Andy and Denny were confident of not getting lost because it was forest tracks all the way, but they would have to find some good cover for the lie up. They'd chosen their ambush site carefully so that if a long line of military vehicles were using the road, they would be able to see the entire length of it which would help their decision making whether to attack it or not. They would only have one chance, so they would want to hit the most productive target possible.

I wished them good luck, told them to take good care of themselves and do a double check on their guns to ensure they were clean as a whistle. I had a special request; could they come and give a full debrief tomorrow to Papa. He doesn't have much to look forward to in his day, but this would really interest him, I said. The more detail, the better. Since my chat with Andy, I had thought differently about Papa. My efforts to engage him in conversation about the events being played out in our little corner of France had improved relations between us. The previous day he had given my hair a ruffle with his rough hand, like he used to do before the accident. I didn't say anything, but it felt wonderful.

Back at the house, we were on tenterhooks all evening. The Germans came and went. I got the answer to a practical question that had bothering me for some time. I asked Papa, reddening slightly, how the two Englishmen relieved themselves up in their camp. Papa roared with laughter and said, 'The same way as the Germans, French, Dutchmen, Japanese etc do it'. Papa was still chuckling when he said, 'I take it you mean how they had a jolly good crap! Well, my boy, it's a good question. What soldiers usually do is find a piece of ground some distance away from where they're camped and dig a hole. They use that for a couple of days, then refill it with the soil to keep the smell and flies away and then move on somewhere else. Let's hope they don't get as far as the backyard outside your bedroom, eh!' On that thought provoking note we all went to bed.

I woke early the next morning. It had at last stopped raining, thank goodness. I was eager to find out how it had gone but Mama told me firmly to leave it awhile. The last thing they would want, she said, after a strenuous and draining evening was a boisterous ten-year-old boy bombarding them with questions. Give them time and space, Mama said quite correctly. Finally, at mid-morning, Mama relented and suggested that I go up to the cave and ask them to come down and spend the morning with us. They must have got soaked through, so a bath would be their idea of heaven. Then we'll have a late breakfast, and they can tell us what they got up to last night.

Esmé came with me on the journey up to the cave. I had a few anxious moments on the way. The return of the heavy drizzle had made the pathway slippery and secondly there was a delay in the response to the whistling of the Marseillaise, if, in fact, that was what it was. It turned out to be Denny's rendition and he was tone deaf. Esmé recognised whose voice had made that sound and was beside herself with excitement.

They both had blankets round their soaking wet uniforms. They were clearly tired but elated. The suggestion of a bath was ecstatically received and that was putting it mildly. After the last bathing incident, they were going to use Mama and Papa's bathroom on the ground floor to which the Germans never had access. They promised to leave it scrupulously clean. The late breakfast idea got a similar reaction. Andy said that the blow by blow debrief would be delivered during breakfast as requested.

Mama had guessed that two sets of a dry change of clothes would be needed, so she had plundered Papa's cupboard. The routine was changed for keeping an eye open for unexpected visitors. On this occasion we needed another pair of eyes to do lookout duty while we all had breakfast, which Philippe Mercier had kindly agreed to do.

We had two new guests for breakfast. The two Englishmen had transformed themselves into two Frenchmen. Or rather, one of them had. Denny looked every inch the Vosgien farmer, Andy certainly not. The latter, being considerably taller than Papa, was wearing trousers that were comically small with bare flesh visible between his socks and the bottom of his trouser leg.

The rich, smoky aroma of that rare commodity, coffee, was sending everyone slightly delirious. Mama laid out on the table slices of ham, several small baskets of bread, other pastries, butter, jam, and fruit. She then appeared from the kitchen with plates with two fried eggs on each. We tucked in. Murmurings of approval and appreciation emerged from our throats. Denny, who had obviously been having some French lessons from Andy, said, 'Myrhiam, le petit déjeuner était superbe. Je vous remercie beaucoup.' We all agreed with Denny's sentiments and complimented him on his improvement. The less said about his accent though, the better.

Finally, we reached the moment we had all been waiting for. Andy whispered something to Mama, and by the way she nodded her assent, I presumed that this was him checking with her about whether she was happy for me to hear an uncensored account of the previous night.

She gave me the All Clear. I had never been so grateful to her. As the senior officer, Denny started the account of last night's events with Andy, as ever, acting as interpreter. By now they were a polished double act.

Setting off the previous night, they had encountered a lone forester on an ancient wagon being pulled by two equally ancient horses. They knew the foresters were fiercely patriotic, hated the Germans obsessively and were considerably more trustworthy than the maquis. Andy, mindful that this man might be a useful contact for getting messages to his colonel, decided that this was a risk worth taking and popped out of his hiding place. The forester was not in the least taken aback at the sight of him nor his submachine gun. He moved his head to one side, spat into the bracken, then spoke to the horses, which halted gratefully. It was immediately clear that this old boy knew of the existence of British paratroopers and said there were some hiding in the woods on the other side of the road that Andy and Denny were going to attack that night.

By now Denny had joined them and cigarettes were passed round. The man was called Albert Cherrier. He wasn't just any old forester but was in fact a Garde de Forêt who was already acting as a go between for Colonel Franks. It was him who had brought the recent message about staying put and awaiting developments. They asked him for news about the Colonel and the Germans. Without a word he kicked off a clog, pulled off a slipper underneath which revealed an outer sock, followed by an inner one. Then, with a bit of a flourish he brought forth a tiny piece of paper that had been wedged between his toes.

There was the answer which he read out to us. We gave our response to him which he scribbled down, placed between the toes, and in a few moments, he was back fully clothed as though nothing had happened. Mission accomplished because, coincidentally, he was in fact on his way to pass the message on.

There was a lot of laughter and back slapping. It was apparent that Papa's opinion of our occupiers was mild compared to that of Albert, whose every other word seemed to be 'les salauds' or 'les doryphores.'

The two Englishmen paused as Papa had something to say. He knew of Albert Cherrier who was a local character and as tough as nails. Papa was amused by what Denny had said about Albert's dislike of the Germans. Mama reckoned he was a safe pair of hands but that his personal hygiene left much to be desired. Apparently, he lived in very modest circumstances which I understood meant a hovel. Mama clearly took rather a distasteful view of him.

They watched as Albert and his wagon continued at their rather funereal pace along the track. The little diversion had used up valuable time, so they hurriedly made their way to the lay-up place they had selected, just off the road.

Most of the traffic would be coming towards them and Raon l'Étape carrying reinforcements, supplies, armaments and petrol to the forces that were desperately trying to stem the tide of the American advance. To start with there was the occasional staff car and motor cyclist. However, they had their eyes on a bigger prize but, at the same time, must not get too greedy. To do so would only end in one result. They must avoid troop carriers because they would be heavily outnumbered.

At last, they saw what they were looking for. A small convoy of two staff cars and two lorries rounded the bend and proceeded along the straight piece of road towards their position. The two paratroopers looked at each other and nodded. The first thing to do was to take out as many of the tyres as possible and bring the vehicles to a halt. Denny stood up, moved out of their cover on to the grass verge in front of the road and fired at the lead staff car hitting the front and rear nearside tyres. The driver tried to turn the wheel away from the danger. There was much screeching as the whole vehicle flipped over, spilling out the occupants. The lorry behind tried to take avoiding action but ploughed into the staff car which had upended itself in the middle of the road.

Meanwhile, Andy had done the same with the staff car bringing up the rear. The lorry in front of it had nowhere to go and so piled into the one in front. The noise of the impact was followed by the screeching of metal as the two vehicles ground their way across the roadway, finally coming to a halt just in front of Andy and Denny's position. The two trucks were still upright but immovably enmeshed in each other and the front staff car whose wheels were still spinning round. Both paratroopers moved forward, knowing what they had to do. The two occupants of the rear car were the first to react, but Denny was onto them, and they quickly succumbed to a long blast from his sten. Andy dealt with the drivers of both lorries, one of whom was trapped in his vehicle.

One of the men who had been in the lead staff car lay motionless on the roadway but there was no sign of the other. Denny watched as Andy moved cautiously forward to check for the man's whereabouts. He stopped when he saw a booted leg protruding from behind one of the wheels that was still gently spinning. The scene was now completely silent. But as he approached, Andy's foot collided with a piece of metal debris. He rapidly took cover as a single shot whistled past him. The man had a revolver. Denny was alert to the fact that Andy needed help and crept around the pile of twisted metal. Two more shots followed rapidly. Denny saw Andy move deeper into cover. By now, they were both in visual contact, and Denny's hand signals indicated to Andy what was going to happen next. He saw Denny standing above the ruins of the jeep behind the injured German soldier. 'Guten Tag', he heard Denny say, providing him with the moment he had been waiting for. Andy took advantage of the German's distraction, moving forward and firing a long burst from the sten into the man's chest. It was all over.

There was a strong smell of petrol in the air. Having carried out a brief inspection of the crash site they discovered they had inadvertently killed a cow which they hadn't spotted on the other side of the road. Their final act was to lob a couple of grenades into the back of the lorries. Under the cover of the loud explosions, the two men beat an extremely hasty retreat. The whole episode had lasted about three minutes.

On their return to the cave, they tucked into the sandwiches that Mama had made for them and downed a couple of glasses of wine, euphoric in the damage they had inflicted on the enemy. It was not just the Germans they had killed they were proud of but also the blockage of the main supply route which would take several hours to clear in the pouring rain. After all that excitement and the fact that they were soaked through themselves, it was no wonder that they had slept poorly.

I was in awe of both these men. I'd never heard anything like it outside of my comic books. I grabbed a broom propped up against the wall and transformed it into my makeshift sten gun. With chest out and legs apart, I stood, mimicking firing from the hip, the broom handle juddering as I made imaginary bullet noises. 'Did it go something like this, Andy?' I asked.

The two men indulged me and my childish display with a smile, but Mama's raised eyebrow was enough to tell me I should put the broom back where I found it.

'How will they react?' asked Denny. My father, who had been chuckling with glee at the boys' exploits, stopped and paused. 'Badly,' he said. 'We can expect the worst.'

Chapter Five

The flurry of excitement caused by Andy and Denny's attack on the German transport was short-lived. The endless drizzle and the interminable waiting for instructions from their commanding officer made for a testing time for all of us. Of course, it was harder still for highly trained paratroopers on a covert mission in occupied territory. Keeping one's spirits up in this situation depended on keeping busy.

It was on one of these occasions that I spent a few happy hours with Denny, who was the practical one of the two-some. He showed me how to fashion and shape pieces of wood with his commando knife which he had been sharpening on a flat rock. He said he'd noticed in our garden a recently felled apple tree which had been chopped up into smaller logs. Denny asked me to bring up two of the smallest logs and a jar of wax.

I came back with all the materials and the lesson began. I had a fellow pupil in Andy who made no secret of his hopelessness with his hands and sure enough, the knife looked awkward in his grip. I admired, though, the easy dexterity with which Denny wielded his. He suggested we make a large spoon for Mama to use in her salad bowl. He'd also remembered Andy telling him that fishing was a hobby of mine and asked me if I wanted him to whittle me a fish. You can guess how I answered.

It was no surprise that carving a spoon out of apple wood was technically beyond Andy. His language deteriorated markedly in his vain attempt to fashion something vaguely spoon-like and by the end it looked more like the kind of primitive weapon you might see in the Ice Age display at a museum. Nonetheless, it was fun to chatter away and marvel at Denny's skill as the fish slowly began to take shape. He ended up making the spoon as well, which Mama was thrilled with. She even gave him a slightly awkward kiss.

Despite the tedious weather, we were a happy threesome during the sessions it took to complete the carvings. Sitting inside the bivouac while the rain pattered down over our heads, Denny whittled the wood and told us stories about his time as a jockey. Once his horse fell at a fence and broke its leg severely, meaning it had to be put down. It was an animal he had reared himself, and as he talked about stroking its face and trying to keep it calm before the fatal shot, his normally calm demeanour cracked, and I could see he had a tear in his eye. I thought that it was strange that he had seen so many people killed but could still get upset about his horse dying. I didn't understand then all the different ways that death can touch us.

Looking back at that time now, I did not want it to end. How lucky I was to have the undivided attention of a major and a captain of the British Army. Sometimes Mama told me that I was pestering them and should leave them in peace, but I knew they didn't mind having me around.

One morning in that period when the rain was particularly relentless, I asked Andy if it was true that it rained every single day in England. Not every day, he said, but sometimes it felt like it. But there was nowhere on earth like England on a beautiful summer's day, he told me.

'I remember one summer when the sun shone for two months without a break. It was so hot that us boys would have to wear these floppy hats that made us look like lampshades.'

'I can just picture it,' I laughed. 'But you lived by the seaside, so every day must have been like a holiday.'

'Hardly, Xavi, but we did used to have some lovely picnics on the beach at the weekend. From the school it was just a short walk across the farmer's field, then down the cliff pathway onto the pebbles. There all the boys were divided into three groups: those that wanted to swim in the sea: those that wanted to play an eccentric game devised by Father that he called 'Spanish he', and those who wanted to catch butterflies.'

My ears pricked up at this. I loved seeing butterflies fluttering around our garden, but I'd never caught one.

'Those of us who were really into collecting, myself included, would always bring our big nets along. Once we caught a fine specimen, it was all about gently putting it into our stink pots, as they were called. These jars had cotton wool soaked in ammonia, rather grim as I'm sorry to say it killed them, but it kept their lovely wings and bodies perfectly intact. After that, we'd pin them onto setting boards for our collection. Living by the coast, we'd often have visitors from your neck of the woods, like the beautiful lemon-yellow brimstone or the painted lady. Those little creatures are something else, let me tell you.'

His eyes sparkled as he spoke and I could see that Andy was no longer in this soaking wet den being hunted by men who wanted to kill him but had taken himself to his boyhood by the sea, a place of happiness and safety. I didn't want him to leave it. 'Then what would happen?' I asked. I'm not sure he even heard me.

'After a while, Father's whistle would sound and we'd dash to the beach where Matron would dish out sandwiches or a currant bun, or what we called an elephant's toenail – a long thin bun with icing on it – followed by a mug of orange squash.'

It wasn't just him that found relief in these memories. Mama and I too said we found these conversations an antidote to the tightrope we were walking. But not for long. During the morning of 24th September, a date I shall never forget, Mama shouted that I was to come quickly. She was in Papa's room and had a piece of paper in her hand. She said that this note had been put through her letter box a short time ago. It was from Aunt Camille and had been hastily scribbled. It beseeched us to get over to Moussey immediately. There was a danger of Uncle Gérard being arrested by the 'doryphores' and sent to Germany. She needed our help!

Papa took the lead straight away and stressed the urgency of the situation: no time for speculation: leave him behind: pray to the Almighty for Gérard and that the car will start. The car was elderly, almost a museum piece, and a notoriously unreliable starter. If its engine noise was frightening and normally disturbed wildlife, its horn sounded like a soul in agony. It was kept only for emergencies because petrol was very expensive and heavily rationed. This certainly qualified as an emergency. Mama inserted the key, took a deep breath, looked up, muttered a Hail Mary, pulled out the choke as far as it would go and finally turned the key. There followed several rather ominously laboured coughs by the engine which finally and reluctantly juddered into life. The noise was deafening but both of us sighed with relief.

The relief was extremely short-lived. 'Merde, merde, merde' said Mama. I looked at her with a mixture of surprise and concern. It was so unlike her to swear in such a manner, so it must be serious. In her haste and preoccupation with what might be about to happen to Uncle Gérard, she had forgotten that to drive a car in the last few weeks since the arrival of the Germans was tantamount to committing suicide. The grey lice had taken all motor transport from us and even most of our bicycles. A cyclist on the road may or may not be a German, but every car certainly was German. Andy and Denny had told us that instructions had been given to both the SAS and the maquis ambush parties that all cars were to be attacked, as all cars were German.

However, the situation was irrevocable. We had to take a chance. Although only a few kilometres as the crow flies, the mountains meant that the journey by road took a tortuous forty minutes. Mama and I hardly spoke on the way, partly because our senses were so alert, our minds racing trying to predict what we would be faced with when we arrived. At last, we reached the village of Moussey, which was rather strung out in the bottom of the valley.

The first thing we saw was a roadblock. We were flagged down immediately by an armed soldier who said in faltering French that we were not allowed through. Mama, who was always good in these situations, said she was a nurse and produced her medical bag and some suitable documentation. Yet another firm 'NON' from the soldier. Then Mama played the trump card. She was here at the request of Major Otto Albrecht. The soldier's reaction was immediate. He saluted and said 'Sofort'. However, before he waved us on, the soldier inspected the boot, we didn't then know why.

There were armed soldiers everywhere but no inhabitants. I looked at houses as we drove slowly past. The noise of the car had brought about curtains twitching and faces appearing at windows. Everybody must be inside.

We drove very cautiously the short distance to the Millottes' house. In the spacious living room, we were greeted by the towering figure of Gérard. Behind him were the three other members of the family. Camille was sobbing, as was Elodie who shrieked from time to time. Maxence wasn't crying but looked shell shocked. It was Gérard who spoke first. 'Thank you so much for coming as quickly as you did. We haven't got long. Let me put you in the picture.'

Over the last few days, Gérard said, there had been a build-up of troops in the village, so they knew something was brewing. At 6.30am that morning, armed soldiers in every street began conducting a house-to-house search. Every soldier had a list of the number and names of each male over sixteen years old who should be residing in that household. Once these names and numbers tallied with what was on their list, the men were ordered out of the house and taken to an assembly point. Gérard was among this group of men, numbering around two hundred, who were gathered in the square in front of the school where they were harangued and accused of collaborating with the British parachutists. The commandant told them that he knew they were harbouring and assisting the British and that an example would be made of them. They would be transported forthwith to concentration camps in Germany. However, he added, he would make a generous exception of those who came forward with information about the location of the parachutists. These men would be guaranteed their liberty. They had until 5.00pm this afternoon to do so. Suddenly the soldier searching the boot of our car made sense to me.

Gerard paused and we all looked at our watches. It was 2.25pm. Two and a half hours to go.

He went on. 'The men of Moussey have all been at

the drop zones and helped move containers of arms, food and other supplies to hiding places in the forest. They've provided shelter when the soldiers needed respite from living in the forests. They know the location of the new British hideout.'

I felt sick. I guessed that Camille, Maxence and Elodie were now contemplating what life would be like without their father and husband. It was obvious too that Gérard knew that these were probably the last few hours he would spend with them. Mama stood up and hugged her brother. Her tears were now flowing too.

Gérard gently moved her away. 'I know the men of Moussey will not yield.' He said with no fear or doubt in his voice. 'The loyalty of this town is unhesitating' He looked at his daughter. 'The Americans will be here any day now, so our time in the ... in Germany will be short. I can be sure of it. You can be sure of this: I will come back.' I had always loved the gentle giant that was my uncle and wished that I had a father like him. But I had never loved him as much as I did at that moment. His defiant and patriotic few words had given us hope.

I looked at my watch. Two hours to go.

How does one spend possibly the last two hours of your life with one's family? Ask Gérard Millotte. It must have been excruciating for the man but with great sang-froid he allocated twenty minutes to each family member for a private conversation. First was Mama, then Elodie, then Maxence and me and finally Camille. When it was our turn, I asked him if he really wanted me there.

'Xavi, hush. I have always considered you and

Maxence to be like brothers. He motioned for us to sit on either side of him on the bench. 'Maxi, until I return, you'll be the father figure in the family. You are growing into a fine young man, and you've got a lot of common sense – more than I had when I was your age. You're getting stronger,' he said, grabbing my cousin's puny little bicep, so you'll have to help with the chores that your mother can't do. Make sure you keep a brotherly eye on your sister, too.'

He told me that I was a good boy and could give Maxence advice as I had had to carry out some of the duties that my father couldn't carry out because of his leg.

"This will not be an easy time for any of us but before we know it the Germans will be gone for good, and we can be together again.' He kissed us both on the top of the head and took us into his enormous arms. That's when Gérard's composure cracked. As he reached for his handkerchief, he looked at us both and said he had one last thing to ask. When it was time to go, he would like us both to accompany him to the assembly point. This was man's work, he said.

While the conversations had been taking place, Camille and Mama managed to pack a small bag – a difficult task when they had no idea where Gérard would be going. They finally settled on something warm: two shirts, a change of underwear and enough food and drink to last twenty-four hours. I glanced at my watch. It was 4.40pm. I looked round at my family. The strain and agony of what the next few minutes would entail was written on all their faces. Whistles sounded. Loudspeakers crackled into life. Knocks on front doors were clearly audible. Mama and I stood to one side and let the Millotte family embrace one last time. I could tell that Gérard wanted to get it all over with as quickly as possible. He literally had to pull his sobbing daughter and wife away from himself as he scooped up his bag and made for the door. He kissed his sister, shouted to Maxence and me to come and left without a backward glance. Mama told me later that that moment would stay with her for the rest of her life.

At the same time, identical scenes were being played out in some hundred and thirty houses in this courageous village. With Gérard holding Maxence in one hand and me in the other, we and the other menfolk followed the line of German soldiers until we got to the square in front of the school. There, Maxence and I had to say our own choked farewells to beloved Gérard who was ushered forwards to join the lines of fellow deportees. We both then withdrew to the other side of the fence around the square to a position where Gérard could see us.

It wasn't long before the counting of the men commenced. Once the junior officer in charge was satisfied that all were there who should be there, he went across to the commandant and another officer who was in Wehrmacht uniform. The two men had their backs to us. They both turned round. The SS major climbed the couple of steps of the speaking platform and started to address the gathering. The other major in the field grey stood beside the platform. It was Otto. Maxence heard my sharp intake of breath and looked at me quizzically. 'That bastard is billeted with us.' I whispered to him.

'Men of Moussey, I hope you have spent these last hours well.' He repeated his ultimatum from earlier. 'Step forward those men who have thought wisely.'

Nobody moved. There was absolute silence. The SS major waited for a minute or so to see if there was any wavering. Still, no-one stirred. You could hear a pin drop. Otto ordered his men to escort the deportees and march them off into the unknown. We caught a last glance of Gérard whose face seemed to radiate defiance. Would this be the last time I ever saw him?

When we arrived home, we told Papa the worst. He was devastated and could only mumble to himself. As well as their own flesh and blood, he and Mama had many friends amongst the good folk of Moussey. As a patriotic Frenchman, his chest swelled with pride at the loyalty and fortitude of the men of the neighbouring village. I told him that it had been a privilege to have witnessed the five minutes between the offer of liberty and the order given for the men to be marched off. The sense of unity and collective courage was palpable. 'Moussey's finest hour', Papa called it.

When I told them both that it was Otto who had helped send them on their way, Mama shouted that he would not step foot in this house again, she would throw him out herself. 'Oh, hush, woman' said Papa, 'do that and we'll all end up with a bullet hole in our heads.' He thought for a while. 'Perhaps you have something in your nurse's bag that you could slip into his cassoulet? Give him a bit of tummy trouble?' For the first time in a while, a beatific smile spread across Mama's face.

'Brilliant' was all she said.

Papa was really getting into his stride now. 'The knock-on effect of all of this is that les salauds will be stepping up their efforts to find our English friends. We've got to be on high alert.'

Mama and I did the usual morning delivery up at the caves. Andy whistled back his few bars of the Marseillaise, greeted us as effusively as ever, kissed Mama on the cheek three times in the French way and gently ruffled my hair. Predictably, both his and Denny's faces took on solemn and pained expressions when we told them the news. Gallant English gentlemen as they were, they insisted on leaving immediately and taking their chances in the forest.

Mama and Papa had foreseen this reaction in their earlier discussions. Papa had said this was the one thing they must not do. To go rushing off into the forest in the heat of the moment was tantamount to suicide. Everybody was rattled by the news but now was the time to have cool heads. 'Tell the boys they must be ready to leave at a moment's notice.' he had said. 'We must assume that this part of the forest will be searched.'

This was another occasion that brought the old Papa back to me, the Papa I knew before his accident. He had always been good in a crisis: focused, decisive, and coolly dispassionate.

While Mama and I had been up with the two Englishmen telling them the bad news and to prepare for a swift departure, Papa had been wrestling with the problem of where to hide them. On our return, we could tell he had had an idea: one that required boldness and had enormous risk attached.

'Les Boches will be searching methodically, but we'll have some time before they get to Pierre Percée.' There was a lot of forest and mountain between us and Moussey, as well as a couple of villages. 'But when the lice get here, they'll find the caves, no question, so they've got to be emptied of anything that suggests they have been lived in recently. Understand? Let's just hope they don't bring dogs, or we're done for.'

Mama and I were Papa's emissaries with the plan. Andy looked anxious. During our absence, they had not been idle. Their rucksacks were packed and placed to one side. The bivouac had been dismantled and was now folded on top of the cushions and blankets keeping them dry from the rain which was expected at any minute. The two rickety chairs were ready to go too. Mama sat down on one of them and Dennis the other. All of us looked at her.

'We have a plan. Let me tell you what Freddy has come up with. But first I need to know: do either of you suffer from claustrophobia?'

The two Englishmen looked at each other in surprise – had they heard the question correctly? They asked Mama to clarify.

Mama then went on to explain in detail about the cubby hole under the dresser in the kitchen where we had put our valuable items just in case the Germans got tempted. Papa was still working on the mechanics of the plan, but needed to know if Andy and Denny were comfortable spending extended periods in enclosed spaces. Papa's own father, my grandfather, had been crippled by fear of confinement for life after becoming trapped in a mine, and he didn't want either of the boys panicking when the Germans were in the house and giving the game away.

Dennis dismissed the question; they wouldn't have been allowed to serve in the regiment if they had a phobia. However, he also said that they would not even contemplate the idea of hiding in the house. If they were discovered, the three members of the Rolland family would be taken outside and executed on the spot. They had already risked too much for them; this was out of the question.

Mama had her answer ready. She explained that although the Germans might discover the cave, the chances of them searching the house where two of their officers had been staying were extremely remote. Otto, after all, was high ranking, decorated, and it would be an insult to him if his fellow officers thought that British soldiers were being hidden under his very nose. She said the least Andy and Denny could do was to come and see for themselves. Mama was hard to say no to. So, scooping up as many of the blankets, cushions and chairs that we could manage, we trudged down to the house. I was beginning to lose track of how many times I had been back and forth so far already, and it wasn't yet midday. My skinny thigh muscles were on fire.

Papa was overjoyed at seeing Andy and Denny again. This was his show and he waved away Andy's protestations about the dangers we would be putting the Rolland family into. He said he knew the German psyche and was convinced they would not search the house because we had obdurate Otto and gangly Günther billeted here. All would be well. What he would do, however, was send me out at the first sign of a search. I was sorry to hear this: after all I had done, I didn't want to miss out. Later I saw the sense in this decision.

I pushed Papa in his wheelchair into the kitchen. There was no problem this time with moving the dresser with two strong soldiers on hand. I can see the two men now peering into the dark cavity. Their cold, dank cave may not have been perfect, but it probably seemed like the Dorchester compared to their new quarters. It was a strange thought that it was only ten days or so since its ceremonial opening with Monsieur Mercier. So much had happened that it felt like months. The fusty, decaying smell was still there, as were their six-legged soon-to-be housemates.

Papa beckoned to me to put the cushions that we had brought back from the cave on to the floor of the hole and suggested to the men that they try it for size. This provided a moment of relief from all the tension. They looked as though they were in a double bed together and when Dennis leant over and gave Andy's cheek a kiss, we all got the giggles. The cavity was about four foot deep, so they would be able to squeeze their rucksacks in as well.

We gently lowered the trap door and left them to it for about fifteen minutes. I pushed Papa's wheelchair up and down over the entrance a few times and jumped up and down on it. I also shouted to see if they could hear us. Then we reopened the door and anxiously awaited their reaction. They were both rather flushed and sweaty. No wonder, given the heat caused by two bodies in proximity and the fact that they were in full battledress. Fortunately, the cavity was sufficiently deep so that their faces had not been pressed up against the door frame and some air had been able to circulate. They had been able to hear voices but not what was said.

Of course, what we didn't know was how long they would have to remain incarcerated and, more crucially, would the air last? Papa thought possibly six hours and, at the very most, eight hours. It would be enough – just.

When they emerged from their new home, Andy asked Papa about its origin. 'It reminds me of a priest hole that you might still find in some large English country houses. They were hiding spots used to conceal Roman Catholic priests who were being persecuted when England was embracing Protestantism.' Denny winked at me – like me, he was amused at the inappropriate timing of Andy's history lesson. He really was a schoolmaster's son.

Not to be outdone, Papa told him that the Vosges, being on the German border, was one of the most fought over pieces of land in Europe. It was no wonder that houses were built with secret hiding places. 'Perhaps the people were smaller then,' he said with a chuckle.

The moment of levity over. Papa ordered the two Englishmen to stay put in the caves overnight but to be ready for a hasty getaway first thing in the morning. The Germans still had plenty of forest to search and darkness wasn't that far off. With that, we sent them on their way. While Mama clambered into the hole with her dustpan and brush to give the space a spring clean (which included a sprinkle of eau de parfum to improve the smell), I made a quick visit to Monsieur Mercier's house and relayed that we might need his help shifting the dresser. Then we waited.

Evening came. Otto and Günther joined us at supper as usual. It was an edgy occasion and we were on tenterhooks: it was the first time that we had seen Otto since the happenings at Moussey; I wasn't sure whether Mama had laced his goat stew with a pinch of cyanide or arsenic. I was terrified by the angry looks that she gave him, and the way she roughly grabbed his plate made me sure that she was going to say something. However, Otto seemed normal. He gobbled down his goat stew, tearing hunks off his bread with his stained teeth and followed it with a belch. Günther looked nervous and preoccupied. Mama asked him to fill the major's wine glass, then probably wished she hadn't. The wine dribbled over the tablecloth. Otto's fist hit the table hard, and he mouthed some obscenities at the poor man. The glasses jumped but thankfully remained upright. Our nerves jangling, we jumped too. Günther coloured visibly and stammered an apology to Mama and his senior officer. He then swallowed the contents of his own glass to calm himself. This man was not born to be a soldier, I thought.

When the major went upstairs, Mama persuaded Günther to stay for a small glass of cognac and gently steered the conversation towards the goings-on in Moussey. He distanced himself from the events there by saying it had been carried out by the SS and Gestapo, who were a law unto themselves. Did he know whether something similar was being planned for Pierre Percée? He thought nothing so dramatic but, lowering his voice, he did say that the search area was being extended to this side of the valley, possibly as early as the next day. He put his finger to his lips and gave us a knowing look. With that alarming announcement, he bade us good night and left the room.

Mama and I remained seated for a moment digesting this disturbing development. She told me the time had come for me to go and stay with Aurélien, but I wouldn't hear any of it. She relented when I reminded her that they needed someone fleet of foot to carry messages. And no one was fleeter than me.

Huddled together with Papa in the kitchen, we devised a plan. Before going to bed that night, I was to go up to the caves and tell the two Englishmen to be ready to move down here and wait in the spinney from 6.00am, the time Otto and Günther usually left. When I went up to the caves, Mama went to the Mercier's house to ask Philippe to be here by 6.30am. We then retired to bed with our minds racing over the plans. Had we neglected to think of anything? Were all the angles covered? Was tomorrow going to be the last day of our lives?

I don't know at what hour I finally dropped off, but it seemed only a short while before the roar of Günther's motor bike awoke me. Andy and Denny were all business when I retrieved them from the spinney. In the kitchen they hauled back the dresser, opened the trapdoor and then laid the submachine guns down followed by the two rucksacks, which they pressed as flat as possible. Denny complimented Mama on how clean and sweet smelling their new quarters were. By now Philippe Mercier had arrived. Hasty introductions were made. As much as he tried to disguise it, we could tell how excited he was to meet the two 'rosbifs'. Kisses, hugs and good luck messages were exchanged.

While Andy and Denny removed their battle dress tops, Mama handed over two large carafes – one full of water, the other empty. This gave us something to laugh about. Then the two men clambered in and lay down. Despite the darkness I could see sweat on Andy's forehead. Denny nodded as the trap door was closed and they were entombed. The final act in this drama of preparation was to ensure that Esmé was as far away from the house as possible. Alas, she could not be trusted to remain quiet during a search and might give the hiding place away of her beloved Denny. She seemed happy enough trotting alongside Philippe Mercier on the way back to his house.

We did not have long to wait. The rumble of trucks pulling into the village square some two hundred yards down the little lane from our house told us that the moment of truth had arrived. These were followed by the sound of doors being slammed shut and the barking of orders and the baying of dogs. I shot upstairs into my bedroom which had a partial view over the square. I could see that the drizzle had started. German soldiers wearing long waterproof capes were being fell in under the instructions of NCOs. I dared to hope the rain might work in our favour, that it might dampen the searchers' enthusiasm.

However, I realised that the presence of dogs made that unlikely. With the aid of my binoculars, I spotted Otto, who appeared to be directing proceedings. He stood on the plinth supporting the war memorial and blew his whistle. He gave them their orders and the soldiers marched away down one of the lanes leading off the square.

Venturing outside, I could see the village was deserted apart from a couple of soldiers guarding the trucks. Where was everyone? I ducked into an alleyway past several houses when I came face to face with one of the soldiers. He grabbed me roughly by the arm and shook me.

'Was machst du hier? Geh sofort nach Hause!' This time I didn't need Günther to translate. I hurried home and this time straight up to Otto's bedroom, which faced the mountain. The view was partially blocked by the spinney but every now and then I caught a glimpse of German soldiers, their capes dripping with the rain, as they trudged up the steep slope. I counted six Alsatian dogs straining at their leashes. The whole search was controlled by a whistle: two blasts for stop, one to proceed.

Nothing happened for three hours. We waited. I was picking at the corner of a crocheted cushion when the sound of a car pulling up outside sharply and sending gravel flying set my hearts racing. I went to the window. It was an official looking vehicle: black and menacing. Worse still, it was flying a pennant with a swastika on it. Mama came over, took one look and hissed one word distastefully.

'Gestapo!'

There were two sharp insistent knocks at the front

door. Mama looked at Papa and me. She ran a hand through her hair, shook herself, took a long, deep breath and said 'My darlings, I love you both very much. Have courage.' Papa muttered. I trembled with fear.

Mama opened the door wearing her most disarming of smiles. 'Good morning, gentlemen, what can I do for you?' That smile might have won over lesser mortals but not the brutal thugs of the Gestapo.

Two figures stood there in the steady drizzle. One was obviously the senior man who could have been a caricature of a Gestapo officer. He was tall and lean and sported a thin moustache, his face framed by small Himmler-like spectacles. His colleague was smaller and squatter. He had a furtive look about him which reminded me of a rat. They were not in uniform, but both wore leather coats and brown trilby hats. There was a driver and another man who remained in the car. The man in charge removed his hat and spoke. 'It's Madame Rolland, isn't it? My name is Herr Lutz and this is Herr Dietrich. We are from the Gestapo. We wish to ask you some questions. May we come in out of this infernal rain?' His French was passable, but he spoke with authority.

Mama ushered the two men into Papa's study. Mama explained who we all were.

Lutz said firmly. 'There is no need for the boy to be here. Send him away.'

I spent the next twenty minutes pacing up and down the kitchen and sitting room, trying to calm myself. I thought also of Andy and Denny lying below me. Before they had been imprisoned in their chamber, we had agreed on an emergency two-way contact system. Three heavy clunks on the floor just in front of the dresser meant 'Unwelcome company. No noise whatsoever.' I had duly clunked as Mama went to answer the door. They must be straining their ears trying to ascertain what the danger was. I was doing the same outside the study door. Voices were raised much of the time, especially Papa's. I prayed that he was not going to lose control. I heard him mention my name a couple of times in connection with the cave.

So, the Germans had discovered it. Fear flooded through me again. Then I heard Mama's clear voice telling the Gestapo men to leave Papa alone and that she had no idea what they were talking about. Moussey was mentioned and I also heard Lutz shouting about killings on the Celles to Raon road. Mama chipped in with Major Albrecht and Leutnant Emmerich's names.

Then suddenly the door to the study burst open. Dietrich hurried out of the house. He reappeared shortly afterwards with the other two men. I was told to go outside while they searched the house. I was sure that terror was written all over my face, were they to look. About an hour later, another car drove up alongside the Gestapo's official car. This was followed by a flurry of activity in the front hall. Hardly able to bear it, I pushed my face against the window and saw Papa in his wheelchair and a tearful Mama standing close by. I dashed round to the front of the house to the area where the dustbins were screened by a fence and peered through a gap.

I watched as my father, visibly distressed, was wheeled out alongside the newly arrived car. My mother followed carrying my father's crutches. One of the men scooped him out of the wheelchair and bundled him into the back seat while my mother climbed in alongside him. Just like that, the car sped off. The dreaded Lutz and Dietrich followed shortly after. I came out from behind my screen and saw the empty wheelchair sitting there all by itself. The front door was wide open. My whole body shook with horror. My hands covered my face and I tried to keep from weeping.

I must have stayed outside for ten minutes sobbing my heart out. Where had my parents been taken? Would I see them again? What do I do with Andy and Denny? Do I give them up to the Germans in the hope that my parents will be released? Suddenly I began to feel resentment towards them. They had caused all this. I went back inside. To add insult to injury, the house was a mess. Les salauds had pulled everything apart during their search.

Looking back at the situation all those years later, I still shudder at the responsibility I had had thrust upon me. I had four people's lives in my hands. What to do? I was a ten-year-old schoolboy with huge decisions to make.

There was only one person from whom I could seek advice. Before I left for Monsieur Mercier's house, I clunked once above Andy and Denny's cubby hole. One clunk asked them the question. 'Are you ok?' One clunk came back immediately. All ok. When I got to Mercier's house, Esmé came up to me excitedly, but I pushed her away. The words fell out of my mouth as rapidly as machine gun fire. He sat me down and asked me to take it slowly. I told him what had happened. Mercier was a big man with the beginnings of a protruding stomach. He was a bit of a gossip which was the reason Papa liked him. He was able to keep Papa abreast of the goings on in the village but on matters to do with our British friends he would die before breathing a word. I was sure that I had made the right call in seeking his advice.

We then went into his kitchen where he gave me a hot chocolate. He was certain that Mama and Papa had been taken to the Chateau Belval, the local Gestapo HQ. He did his best to reassure me that they were just being questioned. However, the tragic events at Moussey did not fill with me with confidence on that score.

The two of us then discussed what we thought the Germans knew. From what I thought I'd heard through the door; it seemed the Germans were looking for a link between the cave they had found and the recent shootings on the Celles/Raon road. In our favour was the fact that the two German officers who were billeted with us, meaning it was unlikely that there would be British in the near vicinity. However, the Gestapo were not fools and could well see it as a double bluff. 'They're fishing, Xavi.' He told me, mimicking reeling in a line.

We discussed what to do with the two entombed Englishmen. Do we leave them there for the moment? However, we were both concerned about the lack of air that Andy and Denny might be experiencing and after a brief discussion we decided that we would both go back to the house and pull back the dresser.

Mercier sighed when he saw the mess. We fought our way through it. Mercier's only comment was 'the bastards' and we made our way into the kitchen. I gave the floor its customary clunk and received a rather muted one in reply. We then manhandled the dresser out of the way and ripped open the trap door as quickly as we could. It was immediately clear that we had got there not a moment too soon. Both men were in a semi-conscious state and distressed by the lack of air. I threw open the kitchen windows and door to the garden. While I fetched two glasses of water, Mercier picked up a tea-towel and waved it about frantically to create some movement in the air. Eventually they started to come to. There was some coughing and spluttering. Mercier had the water ready as they slowly revived. It had been a close-run thing. Papa had obviously miscalculated how long the air would last. However, I had other things to worry about.

After ten minutes, we deemed them sufficiently recovered and so Mercier leant over them one by one, offered them his hand and pulled them out of their imprisonment. Unsurprisingly they were both extremely stiff, so we ushered them both into the garden to complete their recovery. While they were stretching their limbs trying to restore circulation to their bodies and filling their lungs deeply and joyously with fresh mountain air, Mercier and I discussed what we were going to do with them. He told them that Papa and Mama were now in the hands of the Gestapo. They were at once crestfallen, and concern was written all over their faces. Predictably, they blamed themselves and said they would make themselves scarce immediately. Mercier reacted uncharacteristically strongly to this and said a loud and very firm 'NON.' To which he added a long and angry diatribe which could best be summed up as follows 'you're responsible for this mess, so now you must help us deal with it. You cannot just disappear into the forest abandoning a ten-year-old boy who may not see his parents again'.

Denny, conscious of the anger in Mercier's voice, looked at Andy for an explanation. Eventually, Denny said, 'Of course, we must stay and assist in any way we can.'

Mercier, now calmer but still rather sombre, suggested that we play a waiting game and see how things develop. He said, 'All is not lost. The Germans do not appear to have any hard evidence. Let Andy and Denny wait in the spinney, out of the way, just in case the Gestapo show up again.' He literally spat that hated word out. He went on, 'It's unlikely there will be another search. Try not to worry and keep busy. Why don't you start clearing up some of the mess? I'll come by in a couple of hours and we can decide what to do'. With that he left.

Andy looked at me. He put his arm around me and attempted some reassurance 'Your Mama would say "Have faith and believe they will return.". I believe so too. As Philippe just said, try not to think the worst and keep busy. You know where we are if you need us.'

'Try not to worry' was all very well for them to say. The anguish I had felt hadn't diminished in any way. I could not imagine what I would do without my parents. I remembered Mama's words as she went to the front door to let in the Gestapo men. 'Take courage'. As best I could, I started to clear away the mess left by the Gestapo thugs. Keep yourself busy, Xavi, pray that they will be released and try not to think of airless dungeons and firing squads.

I must have fallen asleep in Papa's armchair as the next thing I remembered was a loud hammering at the door and my name being shouted. It was a breathless but grinning Monsieur Mercier. It was his turn to let the words tumble out of his mouth: he had just spoken to Mama on the telephone asking if he could come and collect them from the Chateau Belval. They were free to go! Relief and euphoria surged through my body. I leaped into poor Mercier's arms.

He went to pick them up alone, thinking it best that at ten years old, I should not be darkening the doors of the dreaded Chateau Belval. For the next hour I set about tidying up more of the house. The noise of Mercier's car arriving made me dash outside. Mama was the first to get out. I hurled myself at her and held her so tight I probably risked breaking some of her ribs. She in turn smothered me with kisses.

'Your Papa.' She said in hushed tones when I finally let her go. 'They beat him badly trying to get a confession, but he told them nothing.' Her voice was quivering but I could sense the note of pride in it.

I looked behind to see Papa being assisted out of the car. When he turned towards me, I could see that his face was a mass of bruises and dried blood. One eye was almost totally closed, and his mouth had some gaps where this morning teeth had been. He gave me a painful grin and I could see his trademark gold filling at least was still intact. I had never been so pleased to see it.

'It's good to see you, boy.' He mumbled. I tried to smile but a tear trickled down my cheek. 'Don't worry, the bastards didn't get a word out of your old man.' As he hobbled past me with Mercier's help, he reached out and gave my face a stroke along with a gentle cuff around the head.

Desperate as I was to hear the details of what had happened at the Chateau, now was not the time. Despite my best efforts at tidying, the house was a mess. That had to wait also, as I blurted out that we had released our English friends but only just in time.

Papa was wheeled into the kitchen and Mama instructed me to fetch everyone some drinks. The two soldiers, still very stiff from their imprisonment, reacted in horror at the mess the Gestapo had made of his face. Understandably, both Englishmen said how guilty they felt, that Papa's injuries were all their fault and how they felt indebted to his remarkable courage. My father's reply nearly moved me to tears. He struggled to get the words out of his ravaged mouth. A helpless passenger ever since his accident was how he described himself. He felt he could now hold his head up high alongside his courageous countrymen who had failed to submit to the appalling thuggery of the occupying power.

While we might have scored a minor victory against the Germans, the question was what happened next. The caves would surely be safe again after the enemy's search, so it was agreed we could resume life as normal. As normal as life can be, that is, when you're simultaneously hosting predators and harbouring their prey.

What Papa had endured at the chateau came out bit by bit over the next few days. As I thought I'd heard from the other side of the door on the day of the Gestapo visit, it was the discovery of the cave that had sparked their suspicions. Papa had played the cripple card for all it was worth. Yes, he said, he was a French patriot and had he been fit and able, he may have helped the British, but did they really think that all of this could have been accomplished by his wife and ten-year-old son. His wife already had her hands full being his main carer as well as putting up and feeding two heroic members of the Wehrmacht. The recent habitation that the Gestapo had referred to was in fact his son and various school friends who had camped in there during the summer holidays, as they did every year. The Germans had beaten him to see if his story wavered and out of frustration that it hadn't.

At supper the next night, Papa had made a bit of an entrance to ensure that he made his point about not only having to put up with les salauds eating at his table and sleeping in his beds but also causing him grievous bodily harm. When he was wheeled in, Otto, ever cold and emotionless, said 'Bonsoir', showed not even a flicker of interest and carried on eating. Günther's reaction was different. His jaw dropped and having studied Papa's face for a while, lowered his head in shame.

Chapter Six

In the days that followed, I noticed that Papa's morale seemed to have been boosted by the way he had handled things, but his physical wounds took longer to heal. The bruises on his face went through a spectrum of rather beautiful colours – but he certainly wouldn't be winning any beauty pageants for a while. Meanwhile, the effects of contorting their bodies for hours on end had taken its toll on the Englishmen. Mindful of the risks given what had happened before, we devised a system that allowed them to bathe their sweaty bodies and soothe their sore limbs but beat a hasty retreat if necessary.

We returned to the old routine of me delivering the food to their hideout and Mama occasionally visiting to check on Denny's arm which was still causing some concern. Now the danger seemed to have passed, we began to relax again, slipping back into our previous spirit of fellowship. Esmé too was as pleased as punch to be with Denny again. By now it was getting towards the end of September. As well as the interminable drizzle, it was starting to get colder, especially at night. We began to think of somewhere warmer for the two men too sleep.

It was about this time that Denny asked me whether I had done much fly fishing. I said that I had always wanted to. After much pleading Uncle Gérard had started to teach me using an old rod of my father's. It had become one of my favourite things to do, but without my uncle around I wouldn't be doing any learning any time soon. Denny said that was a terrible shame, but it so happened he was quite adept at using a fly rod himself and would be happy to teach me how to cast.

Later that day I went up to the caves carrying the usual basket of bread and cheese – and my rod. The art of fly fishing, as Denny called it, required patience, concentration, finesse and a lightness of touch. He chuckled, 'no offence, Xavi, but they're not qualities that one would not normally associate with a ten-year-old boy.' You were not using worms or maggots but an imitation, artificial lure to trick the trout or salmon into thinking that it is a nice juicy looking fly and to bite on your hook. The best fishing was done while standing in the moving water of streams and rivers, rather than the still water of lakes.

It was all about the cast, Denny explained, and being able to delicately place the fly exactly where you wanted it: a difficult skill to master and one that would require patience and practice. We managed to find a flattish open piece of open ground – not easy on the heavily forested side of a mountain. Denny demonstrated – with his good arm – the movements required in making the cast with the right rhythm. Under his watchful eye, my fellow pupil, Andy, and I had a go. We were inevitably pretty hopeless to start with, and the only thing I could do was laugh when I managed to get the line wrapped round my neck and Andy, rather overzealous in his cast, caught the fly and hook on a bush.

Denny then demonstrated on a handkerchief he placed ten metres away from us. His first cast was well wide of the mark, the second closer and the third on the money. Andy and I were then pitted against one another. Marks in the competition would be awarded for style and accuracy over five casts each. Each of us in turn took a deep breath, our faces a picture of concentration before letting fly.

Andy somehow managed to land one close to the target and his final one on the handkerchief itself. I, on the other hand, was adjudged the overall winner for my better style despite not getting close to the target. When he realised, he was not the winner, he stormed off in a pretend sulk. What fun we had!

When I got back home later that afternoon, a message had been delivered from Albert, the wizened old forester that Andy and Denny had bumped into on their way to shoot up German transport. When they looked at it, the two Englishmen learned that their commanding officer had on several occasions tried to reach them but between his hiding place and theirs was the same busy supply route where Andy and Denny had conducted their attack. As a result, this road was now more closely guarded. On one occasion the relieving party had to turn back, and another been ambushed forcing them to make a fighting retreat. So, orders still had to be passed by message. Frustratingly for them, it read once again: 'Stay where you are and await instructions.'

The next day, Mama had asked me to go over to Moussey to see how the Millottes were coping, so I bicycled over. As I came in through their front door, Aunt Camille gasped and gathered me into her arms. My two cousins looked forlorn but happy to see me.

'Xavi, I am not sure how I can manage without him.' Camille said, choking on her words. 'The children too, we don't know where he is or what has happened to him, I can't bear it.' She was talking to me as though I was a grown-up and I didn't know what to say, so I let her cry for a few moments. Then, with the effort of somebody dragging themselves out of quicksand, she composed herself, dabbing her eyes with a handkerchief. The words poured out of her in between sobs. 'Our menfolk, they're so brave and your uncle is braver than most. He will return.' Like many of the women of the Vosges, she was hewn from granite.

'Xavi,' she said, after I had filled her in on our news. 'Why don't you take Maxence out for a while? He could do with a bit of cheering up. See if you can raise a smile.' Well, if distraction was what she wanted, what happened next would provide that in abundance.

I grabbed Maxence's football as we left and made our way along the narrow main street. We were just coming up to the school when I remembered the terrible events that had taken place the last time we were there. Before I could suggest retracing our steps, we noticed that something was happening. Groups of SS soldiers were milling about in front of the school gates looking thoroughly sinister in their black uniforms with their death's head insignia. However, it was not that which grabbed our attention initially.

A rotund private in Wehrmacht uniform which struggled to contain his ample girth was emerging from a bakery opposite us with a tray full of what appeared to be meat pies. Maxence dug me in the ribs and we both giggled as 'Fatty Fritz', as we christened him, waddled away in his mincing stride towards the school. He would get some stick from the fine physical specimens in the black uniforms. This was something we mustn't miss. Sure enough, there were jeers and mocking laughter directed at the soldier with the meat pies. It was so good to see the old Maxence appear briefly as he made a reference about how many of the meat pies would find their way into the stomach of the unfortunate man.

It was at that moment that the SS commander appeared and started to bark commands at his men. As expected, they shuffled quickly into rank and allowed Fatty Fritz to continue on his way. There then followed a minute of total chaos and mayhem – glorious chaos and glorious mayhem for us French. It was the only time in my life that I have witnessed combat and every precious second of it remained firmly etched in my mind for many years. I used to lie in bed at night replaying what happened without sound and in slow motion. What happened may get a brief mention as a minor skirmish in history books in the future but to an innocent ten-year-old boy it was much more than that.

While the attention of village onlookers was focused on what was going on at the front of the school, I was distracted by the sound of a straining engine and squealing wheels coming from the direction of a sharp corner in the road behind the school. Three heavily armed jeeps sped into view. Each had twin machine guns mounted on the bonnet. The vehicles screeched to a halt and lined up together facing the school. Each driver forsook the steering wheel for the machine gun beside him and opened fire, as did the front seat passenger with the other gun. The noise was deafening as six heavy duty machine guns near one another started to spray bullets from about forty yards away at the assembled SS men. They all dived for cover except there was no cover, only the bodies of their dead or wounded comrades. Apart from their revolvers, they were unarmed. A few of them managed to fire back but under the fusillade of bullets, it was only a token gesture as none found their mark. Maxence and I had a good view of all the action standing as we were behind the jeeps. It was only after the few stray shots from the Germans that we sought refuge behind a low wall.

It was from there that I noticed that five of the men wore berets but the other one was wearing a theatrical top hat. He must have been in command because when the ammunition must have been nearly expended, he stood up from his position in the jeep and indicated with a wide sweep of the arm that it was time to leave. With that, the three drivers slammed their jeeps into reverse and sped away as quickly as they had come. The whole episode must have lasted a minute at the most. I can remember rubbing my eyes to reassure myself that I hadn't been dreaming. Maxence and I just stood and gawped at the scene of devastation that greeted us as we stood up from our position behind the low wall, not really believing what we had just witnessed.

We walked slowly towards the men on the ground. There were bodies everywhere. Some lay still, some started to crawl away, some moaned. One man's eye stared, seeing nothing, like a fish on display at the market. Another one of them looked up at us, pleading for help, mumbling the words 'Hilfe, um Gottes Willen Hilfe'. Even now in my dreams I see that man, who couldn't have been more than twenty-five years old, staring at my face with bubbles of blood coming from his mouth as he tried to talk to me. Maxence and I looked to see if there was a large grey uniformed body amongst the sea of black ones. It appeared that, despite his bulk, Fatty Fritz had shown a rare turn of speed and made it to safety. However, the meat pies hadn't. They were splattered all over the ground.

We did not hang around to see the German reaction to the raid and ran back as fast as our legs could carry us to Maxence's house. Aunt Camille and Elodie were relieved to see us. They had heard the gunfire and feared the worst suspecting that the Germans had finally lost patience with the village and had gone on some random killing spree. Camille insisted we sit down and talk about what we had seen. After shock and disbelief, the feeling for me was one of confusion. On the one hand, the Boches deserved some sort of retribution for the awful things they had inflicted on the village. Also, the SS were as far as we were concerned the scum of the earth and cold, calculating killers. But having never seen a dead body before, suddenly we had been presented with at least twenty. Scum they may have been, but they were somebody's son, somebody's brother or husband. When I tried to express this to Camille, I could barely get my words out, but I could tell she understood.

When I excitedly told Andy and Denny what had happened, at the mention of the strange headgear one of the men was wearing, Andy smiled and knew instantly who it was.

'Henry's been at it again,' he remarked to Denny who nodded. Andy continued. 'Henry is an old school pal. He always was slightly bonkers. You'd have to be to go into action wearing top hat and brown corduroy trousers. Some people, they don't like his style, but he gets things done without being reckless, which is what our regiment is all about. He's also the most unpredictable man I've ever met, which is useful when you are trying to catch the enemy off his guard.' I caught a glance between Andy and Denny and wondered if they felt ashamed that their comrades were out killing the enemy while all they could do was sit on their backsides. Well, they shouldn't, I thought.

Papa punched the air with delight at the news of the attack and interrogated me about every detail, while Mama tried to shush him, concerned about the effect reliving it all would have on me. After speaking to Camille and Maxence, I felt calmer and was able to put the whole incident in a box in my mind, switching my focus back on to matters that required our attention. There was one thing that made us distinctly uneasy: the possibility of more reprisals on the good folk of Moussey.

I suppose it was inevitable that hearing about Henry's raid made Andy and Denny start to feel restless again. I also began to realise that my time with them would be coming to an end. My parents' pleas for them to stay put and await the arrival of the Americans had landed on stony ground. There had been several narrow escapes which had been too close for comfort, and they had no desire to impose themselves on us any longer. The weather too had played a part in their decision making. The cold nights had made sleep hard to come by.

As we prepared to end this strange period in our lives, everybody's thoughts turned to what we would do after the war and whether we would meet up again. Andy invited us to come to England to stay in the family school during the summer holidays. 'There's bags of space,' he said and looking at me, 'I'll show you Ma Snick's bedroom and the lighthouse opposite at which she used to flash her messages. You can see the wine cask that we rescued from the beach. If you're feeling brave, you could go for a swim and maybe catch some butterflies.'

It was Denny's turn now. 'We could all meet in London first. See the Houses of Parliament, Big Ben, Tower of London, St Paul's and Buckingham Palace. Don't worry about Freddie. I'll be pushing his wheelchair all the way with my two working arms. Then tea at the Ritz: scones, cream, strawberry jam, a cake-stand with fruit cake,

Victoria sponge washed down with copious amounts of tea – or something stronger.' Mama laughed and said she might need a new dress. 'And I would escort you down the Strand' was Denny's response. There was an awkward pause for a moment. Mama's cheeks reddened. Denny cleared his throat and continued. 'Or you can go down to Andy's place for a few days. Then you could come up to the country and watch me and Samson perform at a point-to-point race meeting.' He was getting rather carried away by now.

'Maybe one afternoon, I can take Xavi fly-fishing on one of the chalk streams on the estate and we can see whether we can catch a couple of juicy trout for supper. We can go to Oxford and see those lovely spires. Do some sightseeing, have a damn good lunch at the Randolph and then go punting.'

The two Englishmen looked at Mama and me for our contributions. Her ideas were rather more modest, bearing in mind she had a disabled husband and a brother whose whereabouts and safety were unknown. She thought for a moment and then said 'As I have told you boys, I am a Parisian in my heart. I was born there and that's where I trained to be a nurse. So, to start with, I'd like to take Xavi to see some of its treasures. Then, we would board a train and spend a week in Rome. I must go there at least once in my life to see His Holiness and breathe in the air in the Sistine Chapel.' She added that she would take me to the Coliseum and let my imagination run riot.

Andy said he was fortunate enough to have been there and that we were in for a treat. He then asked me where

I would like to go when peace returned. I had my answer ready. 'I want to go to the sea and sail for days and days in my own boat. I dream of getting a whiff of sea salt in my lungs.'

Andy laughed 'Very poetic,' he said, 'When you come and stay with us, I'll take you out on my father's boat. We'll take your mother too and sleep on board. There's nothing like a stiff breeze to fill the sails and purge your soul of bad memories.' He said with a sad smile.

Conversations with Andy would sometimes take these melancholy turns, and it wasn't until I discovered my mother's diaries that I understood why. I include a relevant excerpt below – she was always a keen observer of the affairs of the human heart...

7th October 1944

Playing cards with A today and he made a reference to a wife! Had no idea – I didn't want to press but the stiff upper lip wobbled for a moment, and it all came tumbling out of him.

So, the wife's name is Mary. They met at a ball in England, he saw her dancing with a 'chinless, grabby fellow' and as soon as they finished, he waltzed straight in, taking her hand and spinning her towards him. They danced six more times that night. A told me she was very beautiful, with 'cheekbones you could slice tomatoes with'. That means something coming from him, as I bet he had all the girls queuing up for a dance! They courted for a time, but the war being the war, things moved quickly.

You can't blame these young people when they must live every moment knowing they could be blown up the next day. Carpe diem, I say. His papa and brothers were happy but warned him about rushing into a marriage. 'Did you not heed their advice?' I asked him. He laughed, 'we were married the next month, in March 1940.'

Ah but his smile faded as he told me the rest. The army liked the cut of his jib (or is it jip? His words not mine!) and he was sent to the War Office but quickly joined the Parachute Regiment – I'm not surprised he doesn't want to be behind a desk as the boy can't sit still for a moment! But it meant he was posted away, and he and Mary would barely see each other. So young to be separated and such strange, exciting, terrifying times, so no judgement from me when he told me that she was seen with other men. But he was not so understanding, and every time they saw each other it was all bitterness and fighting.

But he told me, he's a damned hypocrite because he wasn't totally innocent either. And he let her believe it was her that betrayed him. At this he buries his head in his hands and I can't even tell if he's laughing or crying when he says, 'what a hero, eh?'. At this, I clipped him round the ear. 'Don't be ridiculous.' I said, 'It's war, and you are children playing as grown-ups.'

'Maybe we were too quick', he said. 'But I regret letting her go and I feel guilty at the way I treated her. '

D as ever holds his cards close to his chest. How I would like to see them.

There was something else in Mama's diaries – a theme that seemed to run through her writing during the two months that the Englishmen were with us. During the early days of our acquaintance with them both, I spent most of the time with Andy while Mama tended to Denny's nasty wound. Unsurprisingly, a special bond seemed to develop between the nurse and the paratrooper major despite the language difficulties. She never expressed any feelings for him explicitly, but I could tell from the way she writes about him suggested a growing attachment between them. Although there might have been the occasional quasi-romantic, chaste, non-verbal moment between them, I am sure nothing happened. Tempted she might have been with Papa virtually out of action physically, but her faith wouldn't have allowed it.

When discussions between Mama and Denny became involved, Andy had to be summoned as interpreter. It was on one of these occasions that he was called upon to discover why Denny was down in the dumps about something. There were tears in his eyes. It was obvious that it wasn't physical pain that was the cause because he was always stoical and uncomplaining about that. The English are well known for their reserve and keeping their feelings bottled up inside them. Every now and then, even for these tough paratroopers, something triggers it and all the worries come pouring out.

While incapacitated by his wound, he did not have much to do and inevitably thoughts strayed to home and family. In situations like this, you become rather maudlin and think the worst. Although their position was bleak but certainly not hopeless, he was worrying about his own loved ones and the possibility that he might never see them again. He and his wife, Heather, had twin sons called George and Henry, aged four. How were they coping with all the uncertainty of whether they would ever see him again? Understandably, he became misty-eyed when talking about Heather and the two boys. All this sitting about wasn't healthy for his mind, he said. During these long, dark hours, he had even been wrestling with the dilemma of whether to stay put and await the Americans to improve his chances of seeing his family again rather than jeopardising his chances by engaging the enemy. As soon as daylight came, he dispelled those thoughts.

October 9th was an important date in this story. A message reached Andy and Denny from Colonel Franks via Albert, the ancient forester, that the operation was over. The specific instruction for them was to lie low and await the Americans. The same afternoon was their bath time, so it was a chance for all of us to be together and discuss how this decision was going to affect us.

The baths had lifted their spirits, but their minds were in overdrive. Afterwards, we sat round the kitchen table and listened to the two Englishmen. The door to the garden was open in case a quick getaway was needed. Why had the plug been pulled on their operation? It had to be that the Americans had not turned up, the deterioration in the weather meant that supplies must be very low. After all, the mission had originally been due to last three weeks and by now two months had elapsed. Some of their force of a hundred paratroopers had become separated from the main body (like them) and morale must have been extremely low. So now the operation being officially over, it was a case of every man for himself in a quest to cross the enemy lines. But Franks would have been aware of the nasty wound to Denny's arm and that they were being looked after by a French family which was why his instructions to them were different.

It was clear immediately that this was one order they would not be obeying. They had had enough of sitting around and letting others do the fighting. They were now ready to move on and take their chances like the rest of their comrades to re-join the war. We knew there was no persuading them: they would be leaving the next day. They had already had several conversations with Papa about possible routes to take and decided they would head towards Bertrichamps, just to the north of Raon l'Étape. Papa urged them to be cautious and if it proved too dangerous to return here and try another route.

Mama was tearful that evening when we said our goodbyes. They were going to leave at first light the next morning, almost one month to the day that they had burst into our lives. When we took their supper up to the cave that evening for the last time, they had packed and were ready to leave.

Andy took me to one side. He thanked me from the bottom of his heart for the many kindnesses I had shown them. And then he spoke some words that I would never forget; If one day I am blessed with having a son, and he's even half the chap you are, I shall count myself very lucky indeed.

I managed a few stumbling words myself to the effect that I would never forget him. There was much embracing and tears from Mama as we said our final farewells. Andy did confess to Mama that what had added to his sense of well-being was the way in which she pronounced his name. 'Ondee…th' with the little whistle at the end, apparently it had warmed his heart every time she said it.

She was more emotional taking her leave of Denny. I noticed how much it seemed to pain her to separate herself from him. Andy and my eyes met. He raised his eyebrows and then winked at me. I wasn't sure what to think about that little exchange, which contributed to my growing unease. He made a fuss of Esmé who had sensed something was up.

Before we left, Mama handed over some bread and cheese wrapped in wax paper to keep them going for a day or two. She also reminded them of the simple message system that Papa had devised in case they had not been successful in crossing the enemy lines and were now back in the cave. They would tie a handkerchief on the gatepost by which we used to leave our garden.

I suppose when something like this happens and that which has occupied your every thought for a period is removed, you feel rather empty. Just a day without them had brought home to us how much we would be losing by their departure. Mama had devoted herself to saving Denny's arm with a missionary's zeal and had generally loved the company of her boys. I would be saying goodbye to a confidant, a role model and two friends.

Papa possibly had the most to lose. These last few weeks

had been the most important for him since his accident. He had led the family again and felt of value. He had had lots to think about for once, rather than wondering how on earth he was going to fill his day. His dynamism and resolve – that was the old Papa, and it felt like in the cold empty fireplace there was suddenly a roaring fire. But soon all that would change. The English would be gone, the Germans too and the war with them. He would revert to being the burden. No one would envy him that prospect.

Life did return to some sense of normality, but much of the happiness and laughter had gone. We still had Otto and Günther to feed and house but with them too, there was an end of term feeling about the place. We had not seen much of them in recent days. Some nights they had not returned at all and when they did, it was usually very late, and they had gone straight to bed. The latest information that Monsieur Mercier had passed on to Papa was that our valley and beyond was crawling with Germans as they sought not only to round up the remaining British paratroopers but also, more importantly, was to prepare for the endgame, if you like – the defence of their fatherland. There was much scurrying around on both sides. The Americans too must have paused too in their mad dash to the German border and were now preparing for what they must have thought was the final onslaught – crunch time.

On the third morning after Andy and Denny's departure, I was just about to head downstairs for breakfast when I noticed something unusual out of the corner of my eye in the garden. I literally galloped outside to check it out. It was a red handkerchief tied to the gatepost. They were back! I whooped with excitement, desperate to share the news with my parents. I hoped it meant that they would stay put and await liberation, but Papa was less sanguine. They would certainly try again.

Mama and I took them breakfast. Same old whistling of the Marseillaise. Same old huge grin from Andy but this time also a large smile of pleasure from the less demonstrative Denny. It was Andy who spoke first. 'Just when you thought you were rid of us, Xavi, we've come back to haunt you.' While Mama checked Denny's dressing, they told us their story. They had apparently made good time along the forest tracks. Enemy activity had been minimal. They rested up for a few hours near the village of Neufmaisons until it got dark. At about midnight they made the relatively short journey to Bertrichamps. They would have to cross the bridge over the River Meurthe which was the front line. They found a safe position from which to observe the well-lit bridge and what the enemy were up to. They soon realised they had chosen an impossible crossing point. It had become a major defensive position, well-guarded and bristling with machine guns and other heavy armament. They withdrew carefully and regained the safety of the forest. They remembered an isolated farmhouse they had passed on their way to Neufmaisons which they approached cautiously as there was a light on in the kitchen. There was a middle-aged lady pottering around. The two men looked at each other and guessing that she was on her own and had a friendly face, put their thumbs up and knocked on the glass of the window. It turned out to be an excellent decision.

The lady of the house was a widow called Marie Renault, a fiercely patriotic Frenchwoman. She took them in, put them up in one of her barns and fed them for three days before they made their way back to the caves. It was clear, as Papa had suspected, that the abortive escape attempt had only fuelled their desire to cross the lines. They asked Papa via the Mercier and Millotte families to see if they knew of a trustworthy guide. Papa said that he had a distant relative of his who would be ideal. The next day, a young man called François Locatelli arrived and spent two nights with us. He was a member of the Resistance and was also being hunted by the Gestapo. He spent two nights in the caves. Brave he might have been, but I did not care for him. He was cocky, thought he knew it all and was rather patronising to me. However, Andy and Denny began to question his motives when he mentioned money would have to change hands for his services and said after we had dispensed with his services, they did not entirely trust him.

By now they were getting more restless than ever and clearly fed up. On 29th October, they asked Mama if we could go to Madame Renault. She had obviously impressed them as a capable and resourceful lady and had offered to help if they got stuck. So, we made the journey using the forest tracks where possible. As we got near to her house, we could see the area was crawling with German soldiers. We were stopped by a patrol and asked who we were and what we were doing. Mama was ready for this. She told them she was a nurse on her way to see a patient and showed the officer her medical bag. He pointed at me.

'Mon assistant' she said, flashing a guileless smile. Despite himself, the soldier laughed and waved us on. The sheer number of them made me nervous for Andy and Denny. Mama and I were surprised by how many of them there were in the forests which hitherto had been a virtual no-go area for them.

Madame Renault was only a casual acquaintance, someone we knew from church, but when she opened the door, she pulled Mama into an excited embrace. Finding a guide for the charming two Englishmen to get across to the American lines, she said, would be the greatest honour of her life. Madame told us to leave it with her. She would come and see them in Pierre Percée in the next day or two. 'I know just the person. She knows these forest paths inside out and she's as clever as a bag of snakes.' She said. I wasn't sure whether this was a good thing or not.

Emotionally, this stop-start period was a tricky time for all of us and so it was not surprising that we became tetchy with one another. I made what I thought was an innocent remark to Papa about what life would be like when Andy and Denny had gone. I realised immediately that I had said the wrong thing. Anyway, Papa really flipped. He called me all sorts of names of which the only one I can remember was 'lucky little bugger'. I suppose that related to the fact that he was an invalid, and I wasn't. I did not want that business of him bawling me out without provocation to start all over again, so I said things in the heat of the moment that I shouldn't have, including using the word 'cripple'. As soon as the word left my lips, I knew what I had said was terrible. Unforgivable.

I looked at him and his face was no longer angry. I wanted to say something, to tell him that I didn't mean it and to take it back, but I couldn't even speak. With great effort, he turned his wheelchair round and left the room. I went upstairs and lay on my bed, wondering whether there had ever been a worse son.

As promised, the very next day, a lady who introduced herself as Madame Leblanc appeared at our house. She was an attractive looking lady in her early forties. She had a deep voice and a confident air about her. She had made enquiries in the village about the whereabouts of a nurse whose husband was in a wheelchair and had a gold filling in a tooth. Madame Renault had known of her and that she was already harbouring three other English parachutists in her house near Raon l'Étape after they became separated from their officer as they were trying to cross the lines. We took her up to the caves. She had brought civilian clothes for them to wear although they were hesitant about wearing them knowing they would be shot as spies if they were caught. The Geneva Convention clearly stated that enemy soldiers captured in uniform were under no circumstances to be shot as spies. What they probably did not know was shortly before their mission started, Hitler had issued the 'Commando Order' that enemy parachutists were to be shot immediately without trial, whether in uniform or not, in defiance of the all the rules of modern warfare.

Madame Leblanc then left saying she had some urgent tasks to carry out at Celles and she would meet them at a prearranged rendezvous about ten kilometres from Raon at 6.00pm. She suggested they use the main road because the forests were full of les salauds and she hadn't seen a single one of them during her journey here. So, they left at 5.00pm on 30th October wearing their army uniforms underneath their civilian clothes. We had said goodbye to them on several occasions before so there was nothing more to be said apart from the kisses, the good luck wishes and hopes of seeing each other after the war. It was all rather cursory, but I had the feeling that this time we would not see them again for a while.

Chapter Seven

That night the rain came down hard outside my window. I barely slept, my thoughts with my friends and my nerves jangling about whether they would make it through the lines. As if this was not enough, my brain was playing what I had said to Papa on a grotesque loop. Since that moment we had not spoken.

It was just seconds after I had finally fallen asleep when a hammering on the front door roused me. I tore myself out of bed and went to the window. Esmé was already barking furiously. In the half-light I could see six or seven German soldiers outside.

Mama was drawing back the bolts on the front door. Loud but instantly recognizable voices were raised. The Gestapo men, Lutz and Dietrich, were back. Just the sight of those leather coats made me feel sick. They barged into the house, pushing Mama aside demanding to see Monsieur Rolland. Papa was, of course, still in bed.

They wrenched him out of his bed and forcibly opened his mouth to check the gold filling was there. Typically methodical. Satisfied with their discovery, Dietrich then yelled for the soldiers to come into the house and search for English parachutists. 'Where are the British soldiers? We know they are here.' I could hear the soft thuds of Papa being beaten.

At that moment, there was a disturbance and a familiar voice at the bottom of the stairs. Günther! Was he riding to our rescue? We heard him yell 'Was ist denn hier los? Was machen Sie hier?' at the soldiers who were opening cupboards and mindlessly pulling out their contents. He grabbed one of the soldiers who was pinioning Mama and threw him to the ground. Drawing his Luger, our gentle pianist fired into the ceiling and screamed 'Halt!' The sound brought Dietrich scurrying into the room to see what was going on. I followed on and saw, after a beat, Günther reluctantly place his weapon on to the table and salute Dietrich. Dietrich beckoned Günther into the sitting room, where there followed a heated exchange. I could only guess at what was being said but Günter's voice was the louder one.

It was clear that Dietrich outranked Günther; as we knew, the Wehrmacht always answered to the Gestapo. The door opened and Dietrich disappeared to look for Lutz. A shaking Günther came over to me and whispered, 'Xavi, I am so sorry, but they are in charge here. I told them that they're mad and are barking up the wrong tree. I said that Major Albrecht and I have been guests in your house for some weeks. It is ridiculous of them to think there are British soldiers here as well. But they say they have information to the contrary. I am so sorry, after all your kindness, it should not be this way. I will leave from here and talk to my superiors, but the army is…' he didn't finish his sentence. 'Please convey my sincere gratitude to your mother and father for all their kindness and friendship. At the very least, I shall pray to God that all will be well.' With that he left the house and our lives.

Next door the situation had escalated. Mama who was still wearing her nightdress was screaming obscenities at the Germans and was forcibly being restrained by two soldiers. All the while, Esmé was still barking furiously, which turned into a snarl as she tried to defend her mistress. She jumped up and tried to sink her teeth into the soldier's arm. At this stage Lutz lost his patience with the dog. He pulled out a revolver from his pocket and shot her through the head.

She slumped to the ground. I went down on my knees and fondled her as she gave a brief whimper, breathed her final breath and then lay still. I yelled and hurled myself at Lutz, raining the blows of a feeble ten-year-old onto his head. The other Gestapo man threw me to the ground and lashed out with his foot catching me in the stomach, winding me badly. Papa raised his hands to protect his head from yet more blows and shouted to them 'You bastards have shot my dog. There are no British parachutists here. You searched the house thoroughly before and didn't find any. Why have you come back?'

Lutz said triumphantly. 'Two British men were arrested earlier this evening in the village of La Trouche.

We believe that you were hiding them.' I felt like I had been hit in the stomach for a second time. 'Where are the rest of them?'

Papa denied any knowledge of it, flinching ahead of more blows.

'What piece of manure are you that you beat a defenceless, paralysed man.' Mama shrieked. This remark cost her a hefty slap across the face. Lutz then turned to me as he could see I was getting more and more agitated. 'Stay where you are, Junge. Otherwise, it will be worse for your parents.' He then turned his attention back to Papa who was busy trying to wipe his bloody nose.

Lutz then spat out. 'Monsieur Rolland, I am arresting you for harbouring British spies and terrorists. You will be taken in for further questioning. You can say goodbye to your wife and boy; unless you confess it is unlikely that you will see them again.' With that, his men grabbed Papa and dragged him towards the door. Mama struggled to her feet. 'He's still wearing his pyjamas, for God's sake. At least give him a shred of dignity and let me dress him properly.' She said defiantly. This she was allowed to do before one of the soldiers pushed Papa out of the house. Despite Lutz's words, we were not allowed to say goodbye.

As they left, a soldier with the look of a weasel walked back to Mama, leered at her and ripped the silver crucifix from round her neck. The door was slammed, and the bolt drawn behind us. By now it was dawn, and we were shivering in our nightclothes. Mama took me in her arms and suggested we go straight to the Merciers to seek warmth and refuge.

They were very kind, bathing our wounds, feeding us and listening to our story with patience and sympathy. Later that morning we made our way back to the house, but nothing could have prepared us for what we found. The Germans had been back, ransacking it and looting for all it was worth. The furniture, carpets and crockery were all gone. My mother's furs, jewellery and a considerable amount of cash had all been taken. The trap door to the hole was open. Not content with shooting our beloved Esmé, the bastards had even taken our chickens. A lifetime's worth of possessions, all gone. We had nothing left. But what I saw next had me sobbing: they had smashed up our beautiful piano. The keys were badly cracked, the cover ripped off and the springs split. The instrument's foreleg was broken, and it had collapsed forward pitifully, like a wounded animal brought to its knees.

Mama, devastated but ever defiant, pulled me to my feet and told me that we could live without our things, but we should pray to God every day for the safe return of Papa. With the dramas of the last few hours and the departure last night, I had not had the chance to tell Mama about our blazing row and what I had said to him. I knew he would never talk to the Germans, so I would most likely never see him again. How was I going to live with knowing that was the last conversation we ever had – that he would go to his death believing his son thought of him as a cripple? It occurred to me that his arrest was God's way of punishing me. I had not been able to tell him that I loved him which would be on my conscience for a long time. Mama's reaction was to put her arms around me and hold me tight for what seemed an age. She was emotionally spent.

Esmé's body was still lying where she had died, now stiff and cold. We had told Philippe Mercier about it, and he kindly volunteered to help bury her in the garden.

It was Mama who first mentioned Andy and Denny. What would their fate be? How come within a few hours of their capture the Germans had been so certain that it was us who had taken them in? Somebody must have said something. Mama said and spat out the word 'betrayal'. It was inconceivable it would have been them. Who else then? So many unanswered questions.

The village of Pierre Percée had been shaken to its core, but it said everything about us mountain folk that we helped each other in our time of need. Thanks to the kindness shown by the Merciers and Millottes, Mama and I had beds to sleep in and food to eat. The company of my cousins and aunt kept our morale up and vice versa: they were also praying for the safe return of Uncle Gérard. Through M. Mercier, we managed to discover that Papa was being held locally but moved around. These were anxious times indeed.

There was a strong whiff of liberation in the air. We heard that on 31st October Bertrichamps along with Madame Renault had been liberated. Not for the first time we lamented the two Englishmen's lack of patience: had they waited a few more days, everything might have been different. Then it got closer to home. Raon L'Étape fell on 18th November after four days of heavy fighting, Senones and Le Petit Raon on 22nd November, Belval on 23rd. Now that Philippe Mercier didn't have Papa to share exciting news with, he shared it with us instead. He rather fancied himself as an authority on military strategy. Mama was bored stiff, but I found it interesting.

One afternoon, he sat me down and explained his theories to me. I must say I was a willing listener. The Americans had at last caught up with themselves. General Patton's Third Army had broken out of Normandy. His armoured columns were covering vast daily distances, so much so that by the time he was approaching the Vosges, he was already some 400 miles from his supply bases. For that reason, he had to pause for them to catch up with themselves. This meant that the SAS operation had been compromised.

Now he reckoned that the once formidable German Army was in trouble. What with fighting on three fronts and having sustained so many casualties, particularly in the East, the only way of keeping the Americans at bay in our mountains was by adopting a delaying defensive strategy because that suited the terrain. The steeply sided and heavily forested mountains were not suitable for tanks, lorries or anything mechanised. Instead, there was no other way of fighting it out than by using the footsloggers that were the infantry. The weather had taken a turn for the worse also. The interminable drizzle had given way to much colder weather with heavy snowfalls, thereby making the job of the long-suffering foot soldiers of both sides that much more difficult.

The Wehrmacht had to keep one step ahead of the enemy by using pill boxes, dugouts, dummy fortifications, barbed wire and roadblocks to hold them up before retreating to another prepared defensive line. While there was no doubt that there could only be one winner in the end, each village and town had to be individually captured which of course took time and casualties. Eventually, it became our turn. The noise of gunfire and especially the rat-tat-tat of machine guns got ever closer. The Germans had vacated the strong point of the castle across the valley from the caves. Otto and Günther had been long gone. Our actual liberation was confirmed shortly after by the arrival of two American jeeps in the village square where there was quite a gathering of locals, including Mama and myself. The mayor and deputy mayor were there also and greeted the four Americans enthusiastically. Villagers came up and handed over bottles of wine and local products like cheese, pâté and salami. Mama pushed her way through the crowd and tapped the Deputy Mayor on the shoulder. 'Monsieur Michel', she said rather breathlessly. 'Please tell them about my husband.'

The Deputy Mayor looked rather flushed, possibly excitement or he had been celebrating-probably both. He beamed from ear to ear, slurring his words slightly·as he said to Mama, 'Madame Le Rolland, this is a wonderfully auspicious day for our village, don't you think? It will be a pleasure.' He took one of the American soldiers to one side, a lieutenant with a smattering of French. Mama hovered and was finally introduced to him. She spoke slowly and clearly while he jotted down some details on a clipboard. I heard him explain to her that he was a fighting soldier in the infantry, and it was not part of his job to investigate missing French men, but he would most definitely pass on the information.

Celebrations went on long into the night in the village. Of course, we were delighted too, but just not in the mood to celebrate.

As the war began to draw to a close, many more of the towns and villages around us were liberated. The Germans retreated to their border but there was no more news of Papa, in fact a big silence hovered over us. Mama told me that in the aftermath of a continental conflict, there would be millions of displaced persons streaming in all directions all over Germany and the territories it had conquered. If Papa had survived the war well, we may be reunited. If he had been wounded or was weak and unwell, he might not make it among the hordes of humanity who were all trying to return home or searching for missing loved ones.

The winter of that year was one of the coldest on record with heavy snow and sub-zero temperatures for more than a month. The snow on our roof was piled higher than I had ever seen it and the ice on the lake would not crack, no matter many stones I hurled at it. We feared for Papa more than ever during this time, imagining the frigid conditions in the huts or prison cells where he might be being held.

For obvious reasons it was the least happy of Christmases. We stayed two nights with Aunt Camille and my cousins in Moussey without any menfolk. While the ladies of the village did their best to be jolly for the sake of the children, it was hard to raise any sort of smile and a heavy solemnity prevailed. Mama was true to her word and offered daily prayers to the Almighty for the safe return of Papa and Uncle Gérard. I spoke the words, but I couldn't help thinking about how many people were praying for the same thing, God couldn't bring them all back.

The days continued to roll by, as they tend to do. Some aspects of village life began to return to normality, although for a while yet, the drone of planes overhead reminded us that the war was still not won. I returned to school and somehow the news that we had been sheltering British paratroopers under the noses of the Germans billeted in our house and that Papa had been a guest of the Gestapo had gone before me. I was treated like a hero and even the bullies treated me with some respect. Ah! The bullies! Thoughts about them had never been too far away.

Mama accustomed to fussing around Papa and more recently having four extra mouths to feed most days, suddenly found herself with nothing to do. She remained steadfast in her belief that Papa would return, but these were difficult days for her. Eventually, she offered her services to the local doctor as a district nurse.

The 15th April became a Saints' Day in our family. It is an occasion on which we would speak to each other wherever we were in the world. It was the day when 'that which was lost was found'. For me, it was like any other normal day until I returned from school at about 3.30pm. There were several cars parked in front of the house. The front door was open, and a general hubbub of conversation wafted down the passage to the front door. Just then, Mama's voice sounded above everybody else's. 'Quieten down, everybody. Xavi will be back from school very shortly. This must be his moment.' I put my satchel and coat down. Then somebody started talking again. Mama put her finger to her lips and said 'Shush, Freddy'.

My heart started pounding. I shrieked with excitement and dashed into the room sending Monsieur le Maire flying as well as knocking into his deputy, Monsieur Michel, the man who was responsible for meeting Andy and Denny all those months ago. And there was Papa with the largest grin you had ever seen in in your life. This was a moment I had seen in my dreams, but always awoken to the bitter reality. We embraced and held each other tightly for what must have appeared an age to the two mayoral figures who quietly withdrew somewhat abashed at witnessing such an intimate moment.

I finally pulled away and looked at my father's face. The first thing I noticed was that, miraculously, the Germans had not removed his gold filling. However, after the privations of the last five months, his face was gaunt and pinched and much of his hair had turned grey. He looked exhausted but still physically robust. I could tell almost straightaway that the inner defiance, although dimmer, still burned inside him. We both struggled to get words out or else when we did, we both started talking at the same moment.

It transpired that he had been liberated on 3rd April from the camp in Germany where he was being held and taken initially to Strasbourg where he had been 'processed.' As the allied forces advanced, literally hundreds of thousands of men, women and children were released from prisons, concentration or labour camps. These all had to be identified, accounted for, interviewed, deloused, cared for, given some good, wholesome food, new clothes and especially in Papa's case, a new wheelchair.

During this period of convalescence, he had no means of contacting Mama to tell us that he was safe. He had finally been handed over to the mayor and then, at last, home. He had been moved to different places during the months since his arrest. He had been tortured and beaten to start with but, he wanted to remind us, had never told les salauds anything. Since December, he had been at the dreadful concentration camp called Gaggenau. He knew it was only a matter of time before liberation and thus it was a question of staying out of trouble and surviving.

He had a multitude of stories to tell, some of which we wouldn't hear until years later. While the level of accuracy became questionable after their umpteenth telling, the general gist was that his fellow inmates of the various camps he'd been in had been extraordinarily kind and had taken it in turns to be his daily carer. He had made some good friends. To a paralysed man who had seldom left the house, his life since the accident had been one of predictable routines--and boring ones at that. Despite the beatings, uncertain future, poor food and missing his family, he must have been almost unique in that he had been invigorated by the experience.

What had not been mentioned, of course, was whether Papa had any news of Andy and Denny. It was strange, given that we knew he had been held with a few Allied prisoners of war. Why had he not even acknowledged the men who had been so central to our lives the previous summer? Mama and I even wondered whether he had somehow forgotten or erased them from his memory after everything he had been through. I was nervous about asking him outright – he was so fragile – so I made the occasional oblique references to the caves and priest hole, hoping he would bite, but he never did.

So, we spent the next few days in limbo. I tried to keep myself occupied but my mind kept on coming back to Andy and Denny and wondering where they were. Then, one day, we had a visit from Monsieur le Maire. He asked to see Mama and me privately.

The war was as good as over, he said, and that was something that must be celebrated. Our village had had its fair share of dead heroes but not to the extent that poor Moussey had. Several fathers had not returned after the ignominious capitulation of the French army in 1940. They would be remembered on Armistice Day but, he added, this was a time to celebrate those who had come through and survived.

He broached the subject of Papa's beatings, imprisonment and triumphant return. Papa's story was incredible and deserved telling, Monsieur le Maire went on. He had called a meeting of the village council at which they had unanimously agreed to host a reception to honour his achievements and safe return. Mama and I were both overcome by this suggestion. However, neither of us was too sure what Papa's reaction to this might be. Mama said she would put it to him and see what he said.

When it was mooted to Papa, it was no surprise to us that he said that he did not like a fuss being made of him and all the nonsense that went with it. However, he was deeply touched and, on this occasion, would swallow his pride and agree to it. We all embraced; Mama was tearful, and I just about managed to keep them at bay.

Word went round. Posters were displayed around the village. Everybody was invited. All three of us began to get rather nervous, fearing it would be an ordeal. Mama was worried about what she and Papa would wear. The Germans had helped themselves to most of their wardrobe during the looting of the house. However, reassuringly for us, Aunt Camille, Maxence and Elodie were invited and joined us at the house late in the afternoon on the day of the reception. Camille brought a couple of dresses that Mama could try on. Papa had to borrow a jacket off Philippe Mercier.

When we arrived, we were told to wait outside. We could hear the hubbub of conversation from inside the hall. Then the doors were thrown open and the conversation ceased. I pushed Papa into the hall followed by Mama. Our little procession threaded its way up the hall to unrestrained applause and clapping. I felt myself beginning to well up with pride. These people were saluting the courage and bravery of MY FATHER. We reached the stage at the end of the hall where Aurélien's father, who was built like an ox, lifted my father and his wheelchair on to the stage. Mama and I joined him. I took a deep breath and then looked across at the familiar faces of the families who were still applauding. My gaze moved along the rows until it settled on two boys. They weren't applauding. They were giggling instead. The bullies. While they had been no trouble since the news of Papa's exploits had become public knowledge, I had not forgotten Eric Poirson and Henri Lemaire and reckoned I had some unfinished business with them. I had been racking my brains for an idea to show them that I wasn't a pushover. Suddenly it came to me.

The mayor raised one hand. The clapping stopped and the hall was silent. I looked round at my parents. Papa seemed composed and Mama appeared to be enjoying the occasion. The mayor cleared his throat and began his speech. He started by mentioning Papa's accident and the impact it had had on every facet of his life. Then he gave a chapter and verse account of the last nine months. Unlike his deputy, the mayor was an accomplished public speaker and had his audience hanging on his every word. He started with the two Germans being billeted with us, then introduced Andy and the badly wounded Denny; how we managed to run the gauntlet of our treble life; the close shaves, especially the one at bath time, were greeted with 'oohs and aahs', the impact of Moussey with the searches and so it went on. Mama got lots of mentions and, to a lesser extent, me. The mayor did not skimp on the beatings by the Gestapo, his imprisonment and the whole while my father had not breathed a single word to les salauds.

At this point, the mayor paused while an enormous bunch of flowers was brought forward and were then presented to Mama by his worship. This was followed by two scrolls each lying on a red velvet cushion, the smaller one was handed over to me. I stuttered my thanks to the mayor amidst clapping and applause. Finally, his worship asked once more for silence. He walked forward to Papa's wheelchair with the scroll and cushion where he paused. He looked across at the audience and said, 'Freddie Le Rolland, it gives me the greatest pleasure to award you the freedom of the commune of Pierre Percée. You have made us all incredibly proud of the bravery and courage you have displayed in the face of the enemy. Your actions have enhanced the reputation of our village. I am proud to know you.' He presented the cushion and scroll to Papa followed by kissing him on the cheek in the Gallic way. He then picked up a glass of wine and said to the hall, 'I ask you all to raise your glasses to drink the health of this remarkable man'. After the toast, he asked Papa to say a few words.

I heard Papa start his reply by paying tribute to the two Englishmen who had been the cause of his beatings and imprisonment. He said they were two courageous and heroic men as well as wonderful human beings. He added that their fate was still unknown. Papa droned on, but I wasn't really listening. I was searching for the two faces of my tormentors. They were still engrossed in one another and had not been paying attention. While Papa was still battling away trying to sound grateful and gracious for his award, I took the opportunity to whisper something in the mayor's ear. He wasn't sure that he had heard correctly the first time, so I had to repeat it and give an explanation. Finally, he nodded in agreement. By this time, Papa had finished and there was an awkward pause.

The mayor then addressed the hall again. 'Ladies and

Gentlemen, I have had a request from Xavi Rolland. It turns out Henri Poirson and Eric Lemaire, two of his best friends from school, would like to come up and personally shake Freddy's hand and say thank you for what he has done. Xavi says they have shown a lot of interest in his recent exploits and have prepared a short speech which they are keen to deliver.'

I was staring at the two bullies as their names were called out. They looked shocked and panic-stricken. They had obviously heard their names but were not sure in what context. Their respective fathers went over to them and told them. It was immediately clear that they did not want to do it. There then ensued some animated discussion between the four of them. Both fathers made it clear in no uncertain terms they were to go up and started jabbing their fingers at their sons and then pointing their fingers up at Papa on the stage.

Reluctantly and with their faces crimson with embarrassment, they made their way up to the stage and offered weak handshakes. My father unwittingly played his part superbly by remonstrating with both boys about the strength of their grips. This brought forth laughter from the audience which increased in intensity as he tried on two further occasions to get the boys to shake his hand firmly and with conviction. Their ordeal was far from over because two other voices shouted out 'Don't forget their speeches'. This was seized upon by most of the audience who yelled 'Speech!' in unison in the way people do on these occasions. I later discovered that the two voices that started it all, belonged to Maxence and Aurélien. I was so grateful to my friends for grasping so quickly what I was up to. Eric and Henri looked at each other in horror. Finally, after much throat clearing, Henri, who was the bigger one, managed a few faltering words on how proud the village must be of Freddy and how courageous he had been. That was it.

The boys, their faces sweaty with fright, took the opportunity to flee the stage. I, on the other hand, felt a warm glow of self-satisfaction and offered up a private prayer of thank you to Andy. The prank that he had played on his bully, Farnsworth, had been well organised and thought out. I had improvised. I hoped that Andy would have been proud of me.

After the dust had settled after the reception, we still had not been told by Papa about what he knew about Andy and Denny. However, I was content to wait. I knew that both men were professional soldiers protected by international law and would most likely have been sent to one of the POW camps I had read about. I wondered whether they had reached home by now, whether Andy had found Mary and won her back, and imagined the joyful look on Denny's face when he was reunited with his boys, Tinker – and his horse, of course. Would we all meet again and walk down Piccadilly in the years to come as we had talked about? I believed so.

But I was wrong.

Chapter Eight

It was 1st May and we were all enjoying a celebratory drink. Spring was in the air and much, much better still, the news had just come through that Hitler had put a bullet in his brain the day before; the war was as good as over. We realised that party time was about to begin and the whole country would be delirious with excitement at the prospect of liberty and deliverance from the dreaded foe.

It was this moment, as we were basking in the warmth of hopefulness we had not felt for as long as we could remember, that Papa cleared his throat and said: 'the English boys.' I looked up in anticipation but was puzzled by the grave look on his face. I turned to Mama but her expression was inscrutable. He beckoned us over and I took my chair opposite him at the dinner table.

'It was probably late November, and we were all being held together in a cell in a place called Schirmeck. I think those Gestapo bastards wanted us to incriminate each other, if only by the slip of the tongue.' He laughed without much humour at the mere idea of it. During the time that we had been together, Papa had not got to know them in the same way that Mama and I had. In those three weeks of November 1944, that changed. Papa told us how visibly crestfallen they had been to see that he had been arrested almost as soon as they had been taken into custody. After questioning by the Gestapo, he was put into the same interrogation room as Andy and Dennis. They assured him that they had nothing to do with his arrest.

'The last we saw of them must have been towards the end of November at Schirmeck Concentration Camp: a little black and blue but still in good spirits. The rest I heard from Girardin, a good friend I met in Gaggenau in Germany who had been with them. Andy and Denny, he told me, had been taken from Schirmeck in a convoy of lorries just a few hours before the Americans liberated the camp. Some of the prisoners took an opportunity to escape during the journey but Andy refused to leave Denny – his wounded arm was in a terrible state, the Gestapo had not been gentle.

They arrived at Gaggenau and the likelihood was that within twenty-four hours the worst had happened and they had been taken out and shot. However, until such time as their bodies had been identified, there remained a chance, albeit a slender one, they had survived.

Mama let out an immediate shriek, followed by a bout of sobbing, then started praying out loud. I sat there as though I had been hit by a sledgehammer, then I started weeping also. Papa, in a vain effort at consolation, said that we shouldn't always believe what we'd been told, and we should keep praying. However, I could tell straightaway that he thought it was wishful thinking and they had been executed.

It was a bitter-sweet evening. Of course, it was a dream come true that the three of us were reunited. It was almost impossible to believe that the war that seemed to have dragged on interminably was now over – a war in which France had been humiliated militarily, then occupied and our people, land and institutions had been abused, raped, pillaged and many of our citizens transported never to be seen again or been summarily executed. The architect of these horrendous crimes had now got his just desserts. Peace would break out and life would return to some sort of normality.

Of course, it wouldn't. So much had changed. Nonetheless, we couldn't celebrate because those two Englishmen who had come into our lives so briefly, whom we had loved like our own kin and for whom we had risked and endured so much were missing, believed killed.

Papa then told us how they had been arrested. They had met up with Madame Leblanc at the pre-arranged rendezvous at 6.00pm and set off to walk the ten kilometres to Raon l'Étape, conscious of the fact that she had said that all the German soldiers were in the woods so the roads should be clear. On the way, they passed the village of La Trouche and the local Wehrmacht HQ where they were challenged by a sentry. They were arrested on the spot. The French woman feigned hysterics to give Andy and Denny a chance to make a run for it but, noble and honourable men, they felt they could not abandon her to her fate. A pity they didn't because it appeared that Leblanc 'talked' and mentioned the involvement of the man with the golden tooth which was why our front door had been beaten down at 5.30am the following morning.

Some of the time, Papa had shared a cell with Leblanc and she admitted that the Gestapo had threatened her with all sorts of horrors to her and her family so in the end she had denounced us. They seemed to know about Denny's wound and demanded to know how long we had cared for him. Our friends had bread, pâté, wine and other delicacies in their rucksacks when they had been arrested. There were times when Papa and Leblanc had been questioned together. On one occasion, the interrogator insisted Papa should be wheeled as close to the wall as possible with his hands above his head. The Gestapo man threatened him with his revolver if he turned round while he had sex with Leblanc on a sofa.

For a time, conditions improved slightly. This was because Andy, despite the circumstances, used his persuasive powers to convince the commandant to treat Papa, who was after all a paralysed man in a wheelchair, more leniently. He urged him to reverse the death sentences hanging over Denny and him because they had been wearing their uniforms containing military papers underneath their other attire.

However, that was only a brief respite because all three of them were transferred to the HQ of another altogether more uncompromising unit. They were imprisoned in a cellar and the questioning became more brutal and vicious. Denny's condition worsened and he contracted dysentery. The Nazis used this to their advantage standing on his stomach during interrogation. All the while, Andy tried to care for his companions as best he could. In the freezing cold nights in the cellar, they all snuggled up together with Papa in the middle.

On 4th November, the two of them were transferred to Schirmeck where they met up with another fellow officer from their regiment, Lieutenant David Dill, who, like them, had been caught trying to cross the lines. There was to be no POW status. The three of them were then removed for interrogation, beaten and tortured at the Maison Barthelemy at Saales, the headquarters of a dreaded Einsatzkommando unit. A reliable witness (who later became a friend of Papa's) stated that Denny had been hung up by his hands and beaten so severely that his bones had become visible. Presumably he was chosen because he was the least robust of them and the senior officer. At this, Mama clutched her face and gasped in horror. Papa moved his wheelchair close to her and tried to console her. 'The bastards, the vile bastards', she mumbled. I thought of Denny: his kindnesses: his jokes: all he had taught me. I was dumbstruck.

Papa was brought to Schirmeck on 13th November and was badly shaken by how much Denny's condition had worsened. Despite this, optimism briefly returned. There was talk of the camp being liberated imminently and the conversations of all meeting up after the war resurfaced.

Schirmeck was a camp with endless comings and goings, so new arrivals and departures happened all the time. On the morning of 23rd November, our friends were no longer there, simple as that.

Some six weeks later, on 15th June to be exact, came the news that we had all been dreading. A priest, who got to know Andy during his brief stay at Gaggenau and had survived, confirmed that our friends had been executed on 25th November. Papa and Mama decided straight away that they would go to Gaggenau to pay their respects. I was desperate to go too but was told firmly that this was not something for a ten-year-old boy to witness. I argued but to no avail.

It was now time to take stock of our situation. I wish I could say that life had returned to some sort of normality after the departure of the grey lice and the huge upheavals of the last few weeks. To start with, our house had been ransacked and was now scarcely habitable, our animals were dead, all Mama's jewellery, furs and other valuables had been stolen, our car had been set on fire and was now a burnt-out wreck.

France forgets those who have suffered. We moved into rented furnished apartments, a far cry from the comfortable surroundings we were used to: central heating, bathrooms, a large garden. Worst of all, it was totally impractical for Papa and his wheelchair. Mama now had a part-time job to help make ends meet.

As a family, we discussed in our new impoverished state how best we could remember our two English friends. In our straitened circumstances we felt rather alienated from them and everything that had happened. We decided to put up a plaque at the entrance to the caves which had been their home for two months.

Several months later, Colonel Franks himself came to Pierre Percée and Moussey to pay his respects to the good folk of both villages. He shook us all by the hand, said some nice words and handed over to us an official document testifying to the part played by the Le Rolland family in Operation Loyton. He did confirm to us that the deaths of Andy, Denny and some and twenty-nine other SAS men were being investigated as war crimes. Suspects had been arrested and the cases against them would be heard by the War Crimes Tribunals. He couldn't say anymore officially but you could tell he was hoping they would pay the ultimate price.

Chapter Nine

One late autumn morning in November 1944, a postman swung his motorcycle through the imposing gates of Underley Hall, a sprawling mansion a mile outside Kirkby Lonsdale in the county of Westmorland. The hall, formerly the residence of Lady Henry Cavendish-Bentinck, who had died a few months previously, had become the temporary home of Hordle House School. It had been evacuated some three hundred miles north of its cliff-side location in Milford-on-Sea on the Hampshire coast, which was a potential invasion area.

As the postman parked his motorbike, he gazed in awe at the scale of the house, all turrets and steep roof gables in pale grey stone. It was not his first visit to the Hall – he would sometimes deliver the late Lord Henry's correspondence sent up from Whitehall. But today it was a different kind of missive altogether, but one of no less significance. He had delivered a few of these telegrams in the area during the last couple of years, and his heart always sank as he pulled them from his bag.

He walked up the steps to the solid oak door and rang the doorbell. After a short while, he heard the bolts being pulled back. He steadied himself for what was to come but was relieved when the door opened, and he saw it was not the man he was expecting. It was the splendidly attired and rather ancient butler, Hastewell, whom the school had inherited from its previous owner.

'Morning, Mr Hastewell', said the postman slightly nervously, 'A telegram for the headmaster. I'm afraid it's… one of those,' he added pointing to the words 'War Office'.

'Oh, Lord, no'.

The words hung heavily in the air, before the men heard the sound of high heels on a stone floor.

'Who is it, Hastewell?' The voice belonged to Mrs Barwell, the housekeeper. She took the piece of paper from the butler and looked at it briefly and then took a sharp intake of breath, as her hands clutched her face.

'I should go and find him', she whispered, 'the poor man'. Without saying another word, she shut the door and stalked off down the corridor.

She knocked at the door of the Headmaster's study and went in without waiting for a reply. Ernest Whately-Smith (or 'Whately', as he was called by his seven siblings; or 'Uncle', the pet name given to him by Enid Barwell; or indeed 'The Whale', the affectionate name given to him by the boys) was in the process of lighting his pipe. Through the clouds of smoke, she could see him smiling with the pipe between his teeth, 'Enid, what can I do for you?'

'Uncle, I'm not sure how… Well, a War Office telegram has just been delivered'. She handed the telegram over to him.

His face turned ashen, and he closed his eyes as he took hold of it, as if afraid to even look at the thing. This was the moment that every parent whose son goes to war dreaded. He ripped it open and read the world-shattering message 'Dear Mr Whately-Smith, I regret to inform you that your son, Captain A.R.Whately-Smith 2nd SAS Regt, has been reported missing, believed killed'.

The brevity of the telegram's words belied the immense power they held – words that would irrevocably alter the course of his life and shatter the fragile fabric of his family.

Enid sat opposite the poor man who stared vacantly into space. She touched him on the shoulder and whispered to him 'You know where I'll be, if you need me.' Whately clutched the telegram to his chest as she left the room.

He had to grieve alone but he also had an understaffed school to run. His beloved wife, Dorothy, had died after a long illness some ten years ago. He had three sons, Andy being the middle boy. The eldest, Peter, was in the Royal Artillery and away on active service somewhere in France as was the youngest, John, who was in the Dorset Regiment.

He moved from his chair over to the desk, on the top of which was a photograph of each of his three boys, all in military uniform. There was no doubt which was the most dashing. Andy was taller and more robust and self-confident than the other two. He picked up the photo of his middle son and studied it closely. He then put it against his forehead and the tears started to flow.

He heard a bell, heralding the start of break. There would be boys coming to knock on his door shortly. But he knew Enid would cope. He was used to bad news because there were now some sixty-seven former pupils of his serving their country in every theatre of the war and inevitably some had perished. Every one of those deaths had been a body blow to him but this was his own son.

Of course, he loved his three sons equally. He couldn't have asked more of Peter and John, who were loving, loyal and straightforward. The latter two epithets could not, however, be ascribed to Andy. Over the years he had lost more sleep over his middle son than the other two put together. While he possessed charm in abundance, there had also always been a glint in his eye and a hint of mischief about him.

Whately put the photo down and wiped his eyes. His mind was already in overdrive dealing with the practicalities of the news. He would have to inform Peter and John as soon as possible. And then there was Mary. As far as he knew, the fair sex had not yet played much of a part in the lives of his brothers. Andy, on the other hand, had been very popular with the girls. Indeed, he had already been married and divorced by the age of twenty-eight. Still, he did not relish the idea of relaying the news to his ex-wife.

Andy and his girlfriends, he thought to himself. He had lost count of the number and had often been confused by who was who, with occasional comical repercussions when Andy appeared with them at the weekend. During the early days of the war, he got fed up with former girlfriends or current ones ringing him up to ask for Andy's whereabouts. Then there was the incident at his senior school.

Andy had gone on to Sherborne School in Dorset at the age of thirteen. His highly praised portrayal of Shylock in Shakespeare's Merchant of Venice won him much acclaim, but the other event that marked his time there was memorable for slightly more dubious reasons. Unsurprisingly, it involved a girl. He had been seeing one of the girls from the sister school. When the relationship was discovered, the unfortunate young woman was immediately expelled. The headmaster of the boys' school who had a fierce dislike of the headmistress took a different view of things and made Andy a school prefect and head of house.

Andy was mischievous but it was difficult to stay cross with the boy. There was no doubt that there was always an extra frisson of excitement when he was around. Over the last ten years or so, his visits had been less frequent because of the career path he had chosen for himself.

Better in the real world than with his head in books, he decided against going to university or following into the family business. He reckoned he was more cut out for the burgeoning world of the oil business and the excitement of the United States of America. So it was that in 1937, he took up a position as an executive with The Vacuum Oil Company with special responsibility for France. His ability with the language had obviously impressed his interviewer. When war broke out, he felt duty-bound to return to England and join the army.

This was a happy time for Whately. Once he had got over the stress of the move up north and settled into the new routine, he used to look forward to his sons' visits. These tended to be more special because leave granted to those in the armed forces were usually last minute, impromptu decisions. Often one of his sons would turn up out of the blue. He would never admit it but the visits by Andy felt extra special.

He pulled a large photograph album out from one of his desk drawers and thumbed through the pages of pictures of Andy as a small boy at St Ronan's School in Worthing, then at Winton House in Winchester, and finally at Hordle House. There were holiday snaps taken in his beloved Aldeburgh where they used to spend the Easter and Summer holidays. He smiled through his tears.

After a while, he returned to the here and now. There was hope. Andy was reported missing believed killed. There was a chance he might yet be alive. Whately, of course, had no idea where Andy was, but an educated guess placed him on active service and in the thick of it somewhere in Eastern France or Italy. He might be a prisoner or being hidden by patriotic French or Italians.

First and foremost, Whately was a man of God. He had served for three years as a military chaplain to the Royal Artillery in the Great War and despite being a non-combatant had been awarded the Military Cross and twice mentioned in despatches. So, he got down on to his knees and prayed for the safe deliverance of his son.

He looked at his watch. It was now more than an hour and a half since he had received the telegram. He had to push his missing son temporarily from his mind and concentrate on looking after other people's sons.

This was the way it was for the next few months when there was still no word from the War Office. His influence in the school was everywhere and entirely for good, notwithstanding the burden he was carrying. However, the evenings and nights were the worst time. During term time, he had always been a fitful sleeper, worrying about the possibility of fire in a place where he was responsible for so many young lives. But now he barely slept, and would walk around the school, occasionally looking out the window in the hall and imagining seeing his son trudging wearily up the drive, finally home.

Five months later when there had still been no word of his whereabouts and the war was all but over, Whately resorted to placing a desperate announcement in the Times newspaper of the 20th April 1945 that his son had been reported missing in NW Europe and any information would be gratefully received by his father.

Two months later came the bombshell. A letter from Colonel Franks, dated 13th June 1945: 'I deeply regret to inform you that I have received news from my Intelligence Officer, who is at present investigating in Germany that the body of your son has been identified. I have no further details yet as to how he met his end...'

What Whately was to find out later was that twenty-seven bodies were exhumed from a large bomb crater in the Ehrlich Forest behind the Mercedes Benz factory close to Gaggenau, to the east of the Vosges Mountains and just across the border in Germany on 29th April 1945. Four were subsequently identified as SAS officers, one of whom was Andy. This was only nine days after his forlorn message in the Times.

The last two paragraphs of Franks's letter ran as follows, "After the discovery of an order from Hitler's HQ to the effect that parachutists were to be shot, we never felt easy in our minds…Our only hope rested on the fact that an American official of the Red Cross had been allowed to see Reynolds and Andy on the 13th November but as the months went by without news, these hopes began to vanish. Now they must be laid aside. Both have been identified.

I offer you my deepest sympathy and that of the whole regiment in this appalling tragedy. Andy was not only one of the ablest, but one of the most popular officers we have ever had. We will not forget him.'

While Whately must have known in his heart of hearts that, after some seven months with no news, especially now the war was finally over, his son was lost. Franks's letter of confirmation still broke him.

Andy's death was announced officially in the Times on the 21stJuly. Whately was shortly afterwards overwhelmed by several hundred letters of condolence. Rather than write personally, he chose to send, as his appreciation of their kind words, a copy of a letter published by the Times from Andy's erstwhile employer, the Chairman of the Vacuum Oil Company, which reads as follows: -

'Major A. R. Whately-Smith (Andy) SAS Regiment, whose death was announced in The Times list of casualties on 21st instant, was a young man of outstanding character and ability. As Chairman of the company by which he was employed, I would like to pay tribute to his memory. Andy volunteered for the task through which he met his death. After a parachute drop behind enemy lines, he was eventually captured by the Germans. On at least two occasions he scorned opportunities to escape would have meant leaving his wounded brother officer…His body and that of his friend have now been identified in a Concentration Camp, and so a young life of the greatest promise is now closed.

Andy's service was of the highest order. He was loved by all who were privileged to know him. He will be sadly missed but never forgotten.

There have been so many of these tragedies, that to single out one case for special thought is impossible. I think the greatest tribute we can pay to Andy is to look upon his as symbolic of a devotion to duty and utter disregard of personal safety shown by so many thousands of our young men.'

Snippets of information came in in the ensuing months. He received a letter of condolence from Freddy Le Rolland in which, amongst other things, he said that in the two months they had sheltered them, they had loved Andy and Denny as two sons. 'We knew that the regiment of your son was made up of volunteers who valiantly gave their lives for the nation. They were brave and the Germans were merciless. Do not pity us for our sufferings. They are nothing to the loss of your son.'

He had last seen him on November 23rd in Rotenfels Security Camp when they were separated. He promised to send a copy of the diary that he and his wife had kept during their stay. He apologised for having destroyed the original. When he had returned from Germany and learnt of the awful news, he had become severely depressed which was exacerbated when he was informed that the lady, a Madame Le Blanc, who had betrayed them and denounced Freddy (which led to his deportation) had been decorated for her bravery. This had been the last straw. In a fit of pique he had torn up the diary. At the end of his letter, he added that they had in their possession various keepsakes belonging to Andy which they would send on to Whately. These included his dagger and a silver six penny piece that Andy was always playing with. His wife, Myrhiam, had had it made into a brooch.

Whately was desperate to know more. Not only did he want to know how his son had met his end but also Freddy's letter had sparked his imagination. What had happened in those months Andy was being sheltered by a French family?

Andy's CO had kept his word and informed Whately that he had two of his Intelligence Officers on the ground in Germany trying to discover what had happened. Colonel Franks added that he had complete faith in these men who were 'like bloodhounds once they had got the scent.'

Whately later discovered that the two men in question, Major "Bill" Barkworth and Sergeant "Dusty" Rhodes, were members of the SAS War Crimes Investigation Team and had been tasked unofficially to find out what had happened to the thirty-one SAS men who were still missing and unaccounted for at the end of the war from

Operation Loyton (the official name of the operation in the Vosges Mountains of which Andy, Denny and Diddy (David Dill) were part). Much of their work had to be done clandestinely because the status of their unit was unauthorised.

So, Andy's death was a war crime. Whately clenched his fists so hard that his knuckles became white.

His mind flashed back to the end of May 1915, when he had his first glimpse of his newly arrived son in Worthing and held him in his arms. His poor darling boy had grown into a fine upstanding pillar of English manhood only to be murdered in cold blood.

His mind sped on two years. He was now on the Western Front in 1917 against the same foe and, as a stretcher bearer, he was no stranger to death. He had made numerous forays into No Man's Land to retrieve bodies. Sometimes there were desperately wounded men crying out for their mothers as they clung on to the last vestiges of life. He had done what he could for them, prayed with them and read them the last rites. He had seen what the Germans were capable of as he dealt with limbless corpses, and it had severely tested his faith.

His sons had pestered him to tell them how he had won his Military Cross, but he dismissed it by saying it was for taking whisky up to the troops in the front line. But this was his own flesh and blood. He could imagine the torture and pain that his boy would have been subjected to before he was executed. He hurled a glass paperweight that smashed on the floor and struck the desk with his fist. How would he break the news to his other two sons that their brother had not just been killed but assuredly been tortured beforehand?

The grim confirmation of the bodies being found in the craters and reburied on 13th May a short distance away at a civil cemetery with 'special honours and in the presence of a large section of the population' had arrived in Colonel Franks's letter of 13th June. What Whately never knew was that after Andy and his fellow SAS officers were shot, their clothes were removed and burnt so that their bodies would be less identifiable. It was about this time that Major Barkworth and Sergeant Rhodes came upon on the scene. Barkworth found a body that was wearing a British airborne string vest and also two British identity discs, bearing the name of Second Lieutenant A.R.Whately-Smith. In his report, he wrote 'I knew Lieutenant Whately-Smith and saw him last on the night of 31st August 1944 at Fairford Aerodrome when he entered a plane proceeding on a parachute operation in the area of the Vosges.' Denny and David Dill's bodies were identified in a similar manner. None of this was ever communicated to Whately.

For much of the remainder of 1945 and the early part of 1946, Barkworth and Rhodes busied themselves gathering information, chasing and apprehending perpetrators and interviewing suspects. Finally, arrests having been made, eleven of the staff at Rotenfels Security Camp were charged with killing Andy, Denny and Diddy (as well as three other SAS men, four American Air Force pilots, three French priests and a French Intelligence Officer) on 25th November 1944. They were subsequently brought to trial before a British Military Court at Wuppertal, Germany on

6th May 1946. Proceedings lasted four days, during which all the grisly details came out.

During the final three days of Andy's life, there were flurries of activity around him. On the evening of 22nd/23rd November, the SAS men and the American pilots were paraded and counted in the Entertainment Hall in Schirmeck Concentration Camp. They were then loaded into the last convoy of vehicles to leave the camp before the town was liberated by American forces a few hours later. Dawn the next morning saw the convoy passing through the city of Strasbourg where they again narrowly missed liberation this time by French troops who arrived at noon.

Apparently, several men escaped by cutting through the canvas on the back of the lorry. Not so Andy. He would not leave Denny whose condition had deteriorated markedly following his beatings. They arrived at Rotenfels Security Camp in the industrial town of Gaggenau three hours later. The camp was situated near the Mercedes Benz factory which provided cheap labour to produce lorries for the Wehrmacht. Andy and Denny were put in Hut 3 with most of the other British and American servicemen.

According to witnesses, most of the SAS officers were optimistic and convinced they were shortly to be transferred to Stalags (Prisoner of War camps). The war was almost over, their beatings and torture were at an end, and they could now look forward to meeting up with fellow British officers from other regiments. Only the older and higher ranked Denny had expressed his fears to one witness about the fate they were facing.

The commandant of Schirmeck and Rotenfels Camps was Hauptsturmführer (SS Captain) Karl Buck, a strict disciplinarian who had had a leg amputated after the First World War. He took morphia for the pain in his stump which left him prone to mood swings and terrifying outbursts of temper. The day to day running of Rotenfels was left to Oberwachtmeister Heinrich Neuschwanger, known as 'Stuka' for his brutality. He had a habit of jumping up and down on prisoners he had previously beaten to the ground.

The SS captain (Buck) arrived at Rotenfels on the morning of 25th November with orders for the officer in charge of the guard, Oberleutnant Nussberger. There was a bustle about the place as the fourteen prisoners were assembled in the early afternoon. Andy, Denny and Diddy, the three other SAS men, four Americans and four Frenchmen were ordered by Neuschwanger into covered lorries. A French inmate, Maurice Lesoil, who had befriended Andy, witnessed their departure. He reported that 'Andy left us happily, expressing his hopes about seeing us again soon, free at last. He jokingly said he would arrange a tour of London in his campaign uniform which the SS had marked with white phosphorescent bands on the knees and chest and with a cross on the back.'

Lesoil, however, did not share Andy's optimism, as he had earlier heard that the Germans had asked for a group of volunteers who would be rewarded with a packet of cigarettes and an extra ration of soup per person. Three Russian prisoners stepped forward and boarded the lorries carrying shovels, spades and pickaxes followed by soldiers with machine guns.

This strange convoy then made its short journey to the Ehrlich Forest. They turned down a track for seventy-five yards. When they arrived, Neuschwanger discussed with his two henchmen, Erwin Ostertag and Bernhard Ullrich, how the deed was going to be carried out. They would shoot three at a time and so the order for the first three was given and they were marched into the wood. One of that group was Abbé Claude, the priest of Raon l'Étape. Neuschwanger's pistol jammed at the vital moment and so the priest made a run for it. It is thought that he covered about a hundred yards before he was shot. One of the drivers in the lorries heard two shots with a third some time afterwards. Thereafter, at intervals of ten minutes or a quarter of an hour, the remaining prisoners were taken out in threes and shot until all were accounted for. Each man was executed by the edge of the crater standing by the bodies of those already murdered. Their clothes were removed, burnt and then thrown into the crater along with their bodies. Finally, the Russians were ordered to fill in the crater with earth to hide the evidence.

Some nine months before these events became public, Stuka Neuschwanger was arrested by Barkworth and taken to the scene of the crime. Dusty Rhodes was present and in his own words, '(Barkworth) asked him what his feelings were about the murders that had taken place when the war was practically finished. He just stood there in a very arrogant sort of way. Barkworth turned and looked at me and I looked at him thinking about the people we knew personally. That's when my temper went. So, I knocked him to the bottom of the crater, into about eighteen inches of water that was in the bottom. But he was fortunate because he was coming out. The people that had gone in there before weren't.'

The men who had ordered the execution, Buck and Nussberger, and the men who had pulled the triggers, Neuschwanger, Ostertag and Ullrich were sentenced to death, although Buck's sentence was later commuted to life imprisonment. Dusty Rhodes later witnessed Neuschwanger's execution. 'Right up to the moment he was hung, I don't think it worried him one little bit. I don't think he had any sorrow or remorse at all in him, that man. He was cruel.'

Andy, Denny and Diddy's remains were at last moved to their final resting places in the tranquillity of the Commonwealth War Graves Commission cemetery at Durnbach, near Munich in Southern Germany.

Whately received a 'sanitised' version of the grisly details in 1946 from Colonel Franks. Once he knew that Andy's death was a war crime, he suspected that the details would be horrific, so he was in some way prepared for the shock. Despite this, the callousness of the crime was much worse than he was expecting and again his faith was tested. However, he was worldly enough to realise that the absolute conviction that everything on the Allied side of the argument was a great right and everything on the German side was a detestable wrong was untrue. Having heard from Franks and been reassured by him that

Barkworth and Rhodes were very thorough, he accepted that the perpetrators had got what they deserved.

He did fire off several letters to witnesses to get more information and some replies filtered through over the years. The most precious communication he received was the long-awaited rewrite of the Le Rollands' diary which arrived in 1947. This became a treasured possession to him because of the observations and descriptions of their life over those last two months, both the mundane and the dramatic. He was hugely reassured by what he read. His son could not have been in better hands, and he could feel the love and kindness from the French couple jumping out of the pages at him.

He enjoyed reading about the adventures and scrapes they got into running the gauntlet of the Germans. He still wept periodically reading their words but only because his love of his son and the pride he felt in the way he had conducted himself intensified.

In the end, time was the great healer he had been assured that it would be, and the nature of his job (with a school to run and organising its move back post war from Westmorland to the Hampshire coast) helped him finally to come to terms with Andy's death and the unimaginable horror of the beatings and executions. He would even go on to enjoy well-wishers' bemused expressions when he described his son's last months as that of a troglodyte.

By this time Whately was already approaching his 70th birthday when he suffered a severe bout of pneumonia. Years previously a gas attack on the Western Front had left him with a permanently weak chest; the strain of the recent war had taken its toll and in 1950 his doctor gave him strict orders to hand over the reins. His other two sons, Peter and John, who had been understudying him for years, took on the task. Whately continued to live in the grounds of the school and took services in the school chapel for several years.

The early death of a son or daughter is a chapter that never closes. On 28th October 1951, Whately had to endure the dedication of the beautifully crafted wooden memorial board of the 19 old boys who had given their lives for their country in his own school chapel. Then, out of the blue, came a letter from Maurice Lesoil, the prisoner in Rotenfels Security Camp who had witnessed the departure of the strange convoy on the afternoon of 25th November 1944. Whately received this letter in January 1958, some thirteen years after Andy's death.

Maurice Lesoil was a civilian member of the Resistance who had been captured on an intelligence mission and been taken and tortured in Rotenfels. He came across Andy only in the last few days of his life and the two of them had become friends. His missive to Andy's father had been in response to a much earlier letter sent by Whately. He had tried to write before but had torn up his previous attempts as he was in pieces, mentally and physically, and had endeavoured to put the episode behind him and rebuild his life.

He started the letter as follows: 'November, December, January…the months when each member of the Resistance thinks of his dearly departed comrades. Thirteen years ago, your brave son, dear Andy, was cowardly assassinated, in uniform contrary to all the laws of war. You must not be surprised by my silence …the long, silent return to relative health… I have read your letter many times and reading between the lines I believe I can still hear your dearly departed and I cannot forget that he for all the human wrecks in our quarters was the Captain Smith with courage and faith in the final victory in the future…

When he was questioned at Schirmeck, your son was not tortured (but was severely beaten) unlike other soldiers (Lieutenant Dill had had bones broken in his hand)… Since 1945 I have not had the courage to visit that part of the Vosges for fear that I might avenge some deaths by my own hand… In this new year I ask you for a photograph of your dearly disappeared one, a photo in which I might find that smile he had so close to his death. Please express to the brothers of your courageous, Andy, the piety of my memory and accept, dear Sir, my respectful thoughts and my faithful attachment that unites our two countries." Maurice Lesoil. He became a much-respected professor at Oslo University and was highly decorated for his bravery.

Whately was grateful for this final affirmation of his son's good character. By now, the years and strain of coping with tragedy and running his school in the most difficult of circumstances, together with a weak chest, had taken their toll. Although still mentally alert to the end, he became very frail. However, he had not lost his touch with the young and cheered up noticeably whenever one of his seven grandchildren called on him. Nevertheless, it pained him that he had not been able to visit his son's grave near Munich to say goodbye and tell him how much he had loved him. He died peacefully on New Year's Eve 1963, still in every way very close to the heart of his school.

Author's note

Since childhood I have been fascinated by Andy, my father's elder brother who was killed five years before I was born. Unlike my uncle, I did decide to return to the family business, teaching first at Hordle House and then Hordle Walhampton.

Like so many families, mine suffered badly in the war. My mother's brother, Major Jack Hotham of the Royal Tank Regiment, was in command of a newly delivered squadron of Grant tanks in the North African Desert in the days before the Battle of El Alamein. During a training exercise to familiarise himself and his men with this new American tank to the British Army, they were ordered to clear a minefield when they came under fire from enemy anti-tank guns.

During this exchange of fire, Jack was killed, having initially been listed as missing. He was the only one of his crew to perish or be wounded. This suggests that he was either killed by mortar or machine-gun fire because as commander of the tank and squadron, it was essential he had his head out of the turret. He was killed on 27[th]July 1942. He has no known grave, but his death is commemorated on the Alamein Memorial in Egypt.

Andy, meanwhile, was killed in mysterious and suspicious circumstances in Eastern France shortly before the end of the war. I wanted to know how and, more importantly, why, my uncle, old boy of this school, who gave his life for his country and whose name is on the War Memorial Board at the back of the chapel, came to be parachuted into that part of France and met his death there.

My first memories of him were the portraits and photographs of him dotted around the school where I was brought up. This must have been in 1954 or so when he had been dead ten years. The portrait that really made an impression on me was a large one of him as a dashing army officer in uniform wearing his Sam Browne belt and carrying his cap in his hand.

Over the years, I picked up snippets of information from my father. Not unusually for those who had taken part, he wasn't especially forthcoming on the subject of the war. Mind you, he was positively effusive while talking about Andy and his girlfriends. Perhaps he was jealous.

When I was about eleven years old, my father considered me old enough to have access to the family papers. There in a box file was all the correspondence that had been sent to my grandfather at the end of the war about his disappearance and subsequent fate.

Feeling very grown up, I waded through some emotionally weighty documents. I could feel my own hand shaking as I picked up and read the fateful telegram reporting that he was missing.

It was thanks to my cousin, Anthony, that my interest in knowing more about Andy was rekindled. Ant had become an amateur genealogist and had taken upon himself the task of researching the family history and had traced it as far back as 1543 to the Sudbury area of north-east Staffordshire. Ant had taken time out from this mammoth assignment to exhaustively piece together Andy's mission and what happened to him. He handed over to me an enormous file in which everything was carefully catalogued. This was, at last, a treasure trove of information.

In the decades since Andy and his comrades were dropped behind enemy lines, the SAS became world famous as elite troops. This was not something they wanted. Their mantra had always been to do their job with the minimum of fuss and then disappear as though they had never been there at all. Secrecy and stealth were everything to them. Then in April 1980, an event took place that made headlines across the world and catapulted them into the living rooms of much of the population of Western Europe and North America. I refer, of course, to the siege of the Iranian Embassy in London by six Arab terrorists.

In what would turn into a six day siege, the terrorists took 26 hostages in the embassy, culminating in a high-stakes operation that showed the SAS at their most ruthless and effective. Listening devices were planted to gather intel as endless negotiation attempts continued, before frustrated terrorists threw the body of a hostage out of the front door. As the pressure mounted, police negotiators finally handed the reins over to the SAS. A huge bang signaled the start of absolute chaos as commandos abseiled from the roof amid explosions. The operation, dubbed 'Nimrod', resulted in the rescue of 25 hostages and the capture of all surviving terrorists.

Throughout all of this, I thought of Andy. Although I knew they had seen action during the war, my father, John, and Uncle Peter were erudite and gentle (for the most part!) schoolmasters. How had their brother been one of the first members of this elite group of fighting men?

In October 2000 we were visiting my sister in Austria and on the way from Munich airport we made an unexpected detour to visit Andy's grave for the very first time at Durnbach War Cemetery. It was a beautiful autumn day; the grass was very green and leaves had been blown against the immaculate white headstones. This experience made a deep impression on me as I finally discovered his resting place in the tranquillity of this small cemetery with the backdrop of the foothills of the Alps. Nearby was the grave of Denny, which was also touching to see, and that of David Dill.

A few years later, a TV programme filled in more of the gaps. The rather hyperbolically titled programme 'Nazi Hunters – Justice SAS style' featured the voice of Sergeant 'Dusty' Rhodes telling how he and Barkworth had taken Stuka Neuschwanger to the bomb crater in the Ehrlich Forest and had asked him how he felt about killing Andy and the thirteen others in cold blood.

The point was made strongly in the programme that

the Germans poured in their very best troops to track down the British. The enemy called it with somewhat black humour 'Operation Waldfest' (party in the forest). This included the dreaded Einsatzkommandos, the death squads that were sent in during Operation Barbarossa on the Eastern Front to kill and murder.

I also learnt from the programme how briefly the SAS had gained the upper hand with the arrival of six heavily armed jeeps which had been parachuted in. They carried twin Vickers machine guns and were able to speed along the forest paths cropping up unexpectedly and causing havoc amongst the enemy.

My family and I had talked for several years about a visit to the Vosges. That we finally did it is down in no small part to the encouragement of Tom Pearson-Chisman. I am hugely indebted to Tom. In 2014, Tom who had two children at Hordle Walhampton, visited the area as part of his research into his book on the nineteen Old Boys of the school who lost their lives in World War Two. Through Tom's contacts, we were very fortunate to meet up with two local historians, Gérard Villemin and Maxence Lemaire, which added greatly to our knowledge of what happened, and the poignancy of the visit.

So it was that I presented myself at the front door of 'La Gîte aux deux Lacs' in the little village of Pierre Percée on the morning of 5th May 2015 and rang the doorbell.

***

The person who greeted me was not Xavier Le Rolland,

for there is, I am sorry to say, no such person. Myrhiam and Freddy Le Rolland did not have a son. Xavier and his memoir are a product of my own imagination, based on the very real recollections of Myrhiam herself. The events depicted are all true, but the conversations, scenes (and Xavi's antics) are pure invention.

However, some of Andy's childhood stories are based on truth. Ma Snick really did exist. In fact, she taught your author, and we did think she was a German spy. Similarly, a ship was wrecked on the coast and many barrels of wine were washed up on the beach. An exercise outwitting the customs really did take place.

I have always imagined the day-to-day reality for all those concerned on those forty-nine days, and as a schoolmaster whose career was spent trying to explain the ways of the world to ten-year-olds, the character of Xavi seemed like the obvious pair of eyes through which to view events. It also represented a way to bring into the foreground the French civilians who played such an important part in Andy and Denny's story.

Incidentally, the keen-eyed among you might recognise the unfashionably dressed Englishman from the beginning as a cameo of the author himself.

If you will indulge me, I would like to finish this story by telling you how my family, after a lifetime spent speculating, came to understand what really did happen in that little corner of France in 1944, and to grasp some sense of how those dramatic weeks played out for Andy, Denny, the Le Rollands and the other inconceivably brave people involved.

So it was that in the Spring of 2016, nine members of the Whately-Smith family presented themselves at a hotel in Raon l'Étape, near the village of Pierre Percée and gateway to the Vosges Mountains, the part of the world that had occupied my thoughts for all these years.

Our first port of call was the drop zone, La Pédale, near the hamlet of Veney into which Andy and Colonel Franks had parachuted in the early hours of 1st September 1944 in the north-western foothills of the Vosges, and the Loyton operational area.

We recalled the chaotic circumstances of that night: how the Maquis help had been enlisted to help light and secure the DZ: how they appeared to be more interested in looting the containers that had been dropped with the SAS. They were after food and weapons. One maquisard died noisily after eating plastic explosive which he assumed was cheese. When Andy and Franks hit the ground, they were astonished at the noise made by all the Frenchmen. One of the containers had exploded on impact and several maquis believing the Germans were attacking started firing in all directions. In the chaos that ensued, Andy and the colonel lost each other in the darkness as they fled into the woods before the enemy arrived.

Two days after the events at the DZ, Andy and the other men in his drop were led to a farmhouse near Veney where Colonel Franks was in a meeting with the splendidly named Colonel Maximum of the maquis. Franks was sure that the Germans knew of their presence and on the morning of 4th September he sent one of his men to find a new base near Pierre Percée. During that day, the inevitable happened.

Several hundred untrained and excitable maquis attacked a single truck containing eight German soldiers. They paid a heavy price as reinforcements were quickly on the scene and routed them, killing almost a third of the group.

While the maquis, potential allies of the SAS, ceased to be a meaningful force in that part of the Vosges, it did continue until mid-October to be an effective deterrent to the Germans in rather a strange way. With the encouragement from Franks' men, the maquis managed to keep the vast area of pine forests clear of the dreaded grey lice. They did this because they were untrained and having no concept of fieldcraft, they let their presence be known by using their weapons on every animal that showed itself. The constant crackle of gunfire led the Germans to believe that the maquis had assembled an immense force and in consequence did not dare enter the woods until October.

With the Americans held up, the SAS were now really on their own. That same evening, they had to move hastily to their new base near Pierre Percée as they were informed that a large group of Germans were approaching the farmhouse.

It is, of course, Pierre Percée that is at the very centre of this story. As we approached it, I could feel the excitement beginning to build. On the way down to the village, we stopped first at the ruined old castle that the Germans had taken over at the beginning of September 1944. It occupied a commanding position overlooking the valley that now contained a large man-made reservoir. The village itself was perched on the side of the lake directly beneath us. We could see the pretty square with several cafés, the church and houses. More importantly, we thought we could make out the little lane leading off the square along which was the Le Rolland's house.

But it was the caves we wanted to see. From the back of the house, we followed a path up into the woods which grew steeper as it wound up the hill. Although it was not totally uncharted territory – Tom Pearson-Chisman had been there previously and described the location to us – the track became rougher and we lost our bearings. There were so many moss-covered rocky outcrops that might contain small caverns, how could we find the one we were looking for? We split up and searched, but without luck.

By now we were beginning to feel weary, and our excitement was beginning to curdle into disappointment. It was then that my nephew called out that he had found something.

It was a bit of a struggle for those of us not in the twilight of our youth scrabbling our way down a short steep slope and then up the precarious other side. Finally, we discovered we were on the roof of the larger cave. I was so excited that I failed initially to take in the view. I could now understand why the Germans had used it as an observation post during the 1st World War. It was possible to see right across the valley to the ruined castle and the area to the west was now completely dominated by the lake which, of course, was man-made and had not been there during Andy's stay.

Although we had discovered our Holy Grail, there was no elation from anybody in our group. We were quiet, immersed in our own thoughts. My own were more to do with what a performance it must have been bringing those trays of food up the steep slopes twice a day! That's when the seed for this book was planted.

We each gathered up a piece of rock as a memento. Mine is still outside the back door of our home, so my uncle is never far away from me.

Later that day, we laid one of the SAS wreaths that we had brought with us at Freddy and Myrhiam's graves at the cemetery in the village square. We also laid one at the War Memorial to the fallen of Pierre Percée in the square itself which now included the plaque that Freddy had originally placed at the entrance to the caves inscribed as follows.

REFUGE
DU MAJOR DENIS REYNOLDS
ET DU CAPTAIN WHATELEY-SMITH ANDREW (sic)
PARACHUTISTES DE LA 2 SAS B
FUSILLES PAR LES ALLEMANDS
A GAGGENAU (ALLEMAGNE)

It was in silence we drove to meet up with Gérard Villemin. Gérard is an important person in this story. His father was one of the two hundred and ten men from Moussey who, rather than betray the SAS, was marched off to the Gestapo HQ at the nearby Chateau Belval, interrogated in the cellars and then deported to unspeakable camps such as Auschwitz and Dachau. One hundred and forty of them never returned including Gérard's father. Sadder still, Gérard's mother was pregnant with Gérard at the time, so he never knew his father. He has devoted much of his life to keeping the memories alive of those brave Frenchmen and British servicemen who paid the ultimate sacrifice for their country and way of life.

With Gérard leading us, we stopped off at Schirmeck Internment Camp. Sometime in the previous seventy years on, the area had been developed but Gérard enlightened us as to what it must have looked like in 1944.

Our last port of call on that first day was the village of La Trouche where Andy and Denny were captured near the Wehrmacht HQ on 30th October while trying to reach the American lines. The small settlement had grown and there was now a bypass.

We met Michel Adenot whose father, Georges, had been one of the deportees and as slave labour had worked on an underground Mercedes Benz factory in the Black Forest. He was one of the relatively few who had returned but not for long. Starvation rations had reduced his weight to thirty-two kilos, and he died shortly afterwards.

In Moussey Gérard pointed out the large number of bullet holes that were still evident in the walls and brickwork of the square – the handiwork of Henry Druce and his three jeeps.

On a plaque inside the church bearing the names of the deportees that had not returned, many of them cropped up time after time with at least two families losing six of their menfolk.

Outside in the cemetery were the graves of ten SAS men executed by the Germans. We laid our last wreath beneath the sign which gave their names and a brief resumé of how they met their end.

One moment that will stay with me forever occurred when we visited Drop Zone Anatomie which heralded the beginning of Operation Loyton. When our cavalcade of cars (including Maxence's war-time jeep) drove up, there was an elderly man waiting patiently by the side of the field. Gérard beckoned us over and introduced us to 92 year old Henri Poirson. He told us that he had been there on that night in August 1944 when Henry Druce, David Dill and others had dropped by parachute along with lots of containers. He described how he had lit fires to indicate to the Stirling aircraft where to make the drop. He had hidden behind haystacks and helped carry the supplies to the Jardin David (the first of the many SAS bases). He had been deported to Dachau and then Auschwitz. He rolled up his sleeve and showed us his much faded but still visible tattooed number to prove it.

Our final port of call was the forbidding Chateau Belval, the local Gestapo headquarters, where the deportees had been initially marched to and then 'interviewed' in the cellars below before their removal to Auschwitz and Dachau. I was unaware at that time that Freddy Le Rolland had also spent time there under arrest. At the time of writing, the chateau is up for sale and there is a strong possibility that it may become the long awaited museum dedicated to the memory of the lost men of Moussey and to those of the SAS, the maquis and foresters who had either been killed in battle or brought from detention and murdered by the Germans in the valleys of the Vosges highlands in September and October 1944.

Moved by the generosity and kindness they had

showed us, we bade goodbye to our new friends. And so, after sixty years, journey's end. On the way home, I felt that a void in my life had gone some way to being filled. In November when we have the official Remembrance Day service at my grandfather's school and the names of the fallen are read out, my thoughts will flicker between those portraits in my family home, that gravestone in the beautiful cemetery overlooking the Alps, the Gîte aux deux lacs in the village of Pierre Percée and those two caves up the mountainside beyond it.

Calculating the number of dead from the Second World War is incredibly difficult, but some statisticians estimate it at approximately 50 million. My family's experience, then, is far from unique. But it has been a privilege to tell the story of a small group of those who paid the ultimate sacrifice for their service to their country and their fellow man.

Acknowledgements

Apart from the assistance from Anthony Whately-Smith, Tom Pearson-Chisman and Gerard Villemin, to which I have already alluded, I should like to add my thanks to Sarah Prunier-Duparge who was a charming and knowledgeable host to the four Whately-Smith men on our most recent visit to Pierre-Percée and Moussey in May 2022.

I would also like to thank my neurologist, Dr Peter Bain MBBS MA(Oxon) MD FRCP, for reading my book and contributing to the foreword. As a Parkinson's sufferer, I much value my sessions with him, as well as his positivity.

Thanks also to Keith Burns for allowing me to use his atmospheric painting 'Descend to Defend' as the cover for my book. I should also like to express my gratitude to the charity responsible for commissioning the painting and erecting the memorials, the SAS and LRDG Roll of Honour (sas-lrdg-roh.com)

Finally, I should like to thank my brother, Jos, for all his encouragement and, most of all, my son, Charlie, who is not only a Whately-Smith but also a wordsmith. As my editor, he has brought his professional experience to bear, advising me on things like narrative structure, characterisation and prose style.

Sources

Unpublished reports, memoirs, papers

Freddie and Myrhiam le Rolland diary of September, October and November 1944.

Private papers belonging to the Whately-Smith family.

Report on Operation Loyton by Colonel Franks M.C.

Reports on the missing SAS personnel captured by the Germans in Eastern France in Autumn 1944 (including the Gaggenau atrocity).

Published Sources

The Founding of Hordle House by P.G.Whately-Smith

Remembrance by Tom Pearson-Chisman

Four Studies in Loyalty by Christopher Sykes

SAS Band of Brothers by Damien Lewis

Rudi's Story – The diary and wartime experiences of Rudolf Friedlaender by Gerhart Friedlander and Keith Turner

Film Footage, TV etc
Yesterday Channel, The Nazi Hunters, Justice – SAS style